A DIAMOND
BEFORE
YOU DIE

Other Books by Chris Wiltz

THE KILLING CIRCLE

A DIAMOND
BEFORE
YOU DIE

CHRIS WILTZ

THE MYSTERIOUS PRESS • New York

The Mysterious Press, 129 West 56th Street, New York, N.Y. 10019

Printed in the United States of America
First Printing: April 1987
10 9 8 7 6 5 4 3 2 1

Library of Congress Cataloging-in-Publication Data

Wiltz, Chris.
    A diamond before you die.

    I. Title.
PS3573.I4783D5   1987   813'.54   86-62776
ISBN 0-89296-192-9

For Joe

CONTENTS

1

The Man
in the Fireplace

I went over to Richard Cotton's house that night to tell him I'd followed his wife out to the airport and seen her get on a plane going to Mexico City. The part I supposed he'd be most interested in was that she'd been alone.

His Mercedes wasn't in the driveway, but it could have been in the garage so I went to the door anyway. I was ringing the doorbell for the second time when I heard a crash.

"Richard!" I yelled, and started shaking the doorknob and pounding on the door.

I ran across the porch to the living room windows—floor to ceiling, double-hung French windows. They were too heavily curtained to see through. I put my ear up to a pane of glass. The sounds were muffled, but there was a struggle going on inside. I tried the windows knowing they'd be locked, then I listened again. This time I heard nothing, and that sounded even more ominous. I went back to the door and tried to kick it in, but my legs were going to splinter before that double-bolted solid oak did. So I ran down the porch, picked up a small wrought-iron chair and pitched it through a window.

What I saw and heard when I stumbled past drapes, wing chairs and tiny tables toward the flickering firelight was almost too much to take in at once. There were the hissing sounds a fire makes

1

when something wet hits it; there was a sickening smell that my mind fought against identifying. And there was a woman standing there watching a man roast in the fireplace.

It was the man's head that was roasting, actually. The rest of his body, twisted from writhing, lay across the hearth and the rug, part of the collapsed fireplace screen underneath him. He had a death-tight grip on the poker.

I recovered from the assault on my senses, got past a long sofa and some other furniture, and pulled him out of the fire by his ankles. Only the sight of his raw, blistered face made the woman stop looking at him and look at me.

"What were you going to do, let him burn to death?" I asked her angrily.

I turned the lights on, found a phone and called for a crash truck and the cops.

Her name was Lee Diamond. When I returned to the living room she was still standing over the man who didn't have much of a face left. I asked her what she was doing in Cotton's house, and as she turned her head to answer, her face contracted in a spasm of pain. Her hand went up to hold the side of her neck. I had to step over the burned man's legs to get to her. Under the cowl of her thick sweater, at the base of her neck, above her left shoulder, was a very ugly mark, inflamed and swelling. I tested the sponginess over her collarbone to see if it was broken, but with a swift and surprisingly strong movement she flung my hand away from her. She started moving toward the sofa, stumbling on the man's leg, then on me. She resisted my help at first, but leaned into me as I got her past the obstacles, which included an overturned end table and shattered lamp. She sunk into the sofa cushions, holding her neck again.

A patrol car arrived first, followed closely by the paramedics. Detective Lieutenant Roderick Rankin and his sidekick Phil Fonte brought up the rear. I'd put a special call in to Rankin because he's my old man's best friend and would have expected me to, and because if this was an attempted homicide he would have been there anyway. Usually when Uncle Roddy and I meet in any kind of professional capacity he has a few snide words for me—I've come to regard this as his way of showing me affection when he's surrounded by his subordinates—but not this time. This time the burn victim's presence cut short any cute exchanges. Uncle Roddy put himself and his men at the paramedics' disposal while they did what they had to, though he did tell Fonte to go check the rest of the place. I told Uncle Roddy that the lady might have a broken collarbone, and I went into the kitchen to make an ice pack. When I came back, I was relieved to see the paramedics wheeling the man away on a stretcher.

Lee Diamond was saying that she didn't want to go in the crash truck, that she didn't think her collarbone was broken, that she'd rather go to Touro Infirmary than Charity Hospital, which was where they were taking the burned man.

She stopped Uncle Roddy's attempt to get her immediate medical attention. "I'd rather answer all of your questions right here, right now, Lieutenant." She shuddered when I put the ice pack down inside the cowl.

She said the man tried to kill her. She'd been sitting outside the house in her car when she thought she saw the front door open. None of the outside lights were on in the front, so she got out of the car to see what was going on. She crept down behind the hedges in the shadow of some azalea bushes. Almost immediately the man jumped her. He strong-armed her into the house with an effective throat hold and shoved her into the living room. That's when she started fighting back. They grappled with each other for a while, upsetting the table, smashing the lamp, and then he swung the poker at her.

This was some strong woman, because even after the blow she'd taken, she managed to knee him in the groin with enough force that he fell back, struck his head on the fireplace bricks, and continued falling into the fire.

She didn't appear to be particularly strong. Her height was average and so was her build. I took her to be in her early thirties, but in tight black jeans and that big sweater she could have been a little on the slight side, both of build and age—probably about thirty. Her hair was brown, shoulder length, and her eyes were hazel, almost yellow in the firelight, just hazel once I'd turned on the living room lights.

But if you think this is the ordinary description of some ordinary woman, let me tell you she was not, and it had nothing so much to do with her looks. She was good-looking all right, but what was not at all ordinary was the way she carried herself, even with the injury, even when she was stumbling. There was a readiness about her, a tenseness, but it was very quiet, very cool. It had nothing to do with being nervous or anxious. It had nothing whatsoever to do with any kind of performance or any kind of impression she was trying to create.

My guess, in fact, was that she could blend in anywhere, become nearly invisible and seem very ordinary. But not if she didn't want to, not if she was focused on you. What was not ordinary at all was the way she could get you to react to her, and then, as I found out later, if she wanted to, make you change your reaction.

Already Uncle Roddy was at bay.

"Miss Diamond," he said so nicely, "what exactly were you doing sitting outside the house in your car?" Uncle Roddy's best smile is usually a grimace or a sardonic leer, but the way his fat cheeks were folded back on his big face right now was something to see. Uncle Roddy was smiling to beat the band. His normally dopey-looking eyes still had their lids halfway down, but there were these little crinkles all around them that I'd never seen before, and I don't remember when I didn't know Uncle Roddy.

"Just what you would think, Lieutenant," she said. "I was staking out the house." There was not a hint of patronization or sarcasm in her voice. She was businesslike.

"Are you licensed as a private detective, Miss Diamond?"

"Yes."

"Then I'm sure you know how helpful it would be if you would elaborate."

"I do, Lieutenant, and I'm sure you know that total elaboration is not always possible. I'm not free to elaborate."

If I had handed Uncle Roddy that elaboration line, he'd be threatening to take my license away.

"Can you tell me who your client is?" he asked her instead.

"I'm not free to tell you that."

By now Uncle Roddy would have me on the way to jail for withholding evidence. But all he said to her was, "Can you get in touch with your client quickly, Miss Diamond, as soon as you get that injury taken care of?"

"My client is out of the country. There will be some delay."

"Where is your client?"

She said with such calm, "I'm not free to tell you that. What I can tell you, Lieutenant, is that I've been staking out this house off and on for a couple of weeks, and I've never seen that man here before." I tell you there was not a hint of ingratiation.

Fonte walked in while she was giving Uncle Roddy this handsome bit of information.

"No sign of forced entry, Lieutenant. There's another house out back but it's dark and all locked up."

The first flash of irritation crossed Uncle Roddy's face. "All right, Fonte." Then, "Miss Diamond, let's talk about all this tomorrow after you've made sure your collarbone's in one piece. Sergeant Fonte will see that you get to the hospital."

It seemed to me that Uncle Roddy wanted Fonte out of the way for a while, though he'd taken Fonte under his wing much the same way my father had taken Uncle Roddy under his thirty-plus years ago. But this partnership wasn't charmed the way the Rankin-Rafferty partnership had been. Of course, those two men were a lot closer in age; Fonte's of another generation. And it's true that the old man is probably the only person in the world who doesn't irritate Uncle Roddy. They like to sit around together, drinking beer and talking about the old days and how they don't make cops the way they used to. They're usually talking about the incompetents on the force, but I've been used as an example to bear out this statement since I managed to get myself thrown off the force because of the Angelesi–Myra Ledet business. I wonder how many times I've been told that any other cop in the city of

New Orleans would have known when to close his eyes and when to open them again.

"Fine, Lieutenant," Lee Diamond said. She let Uncle Roddy help her up from the sofa. She smiled at him, told him she'd be in his office first thing in the morning, then she turned around and thanked me before she left with Fonte.

"Jesus, it's hot in here," Uncle Roddy said. "Let's get some windows open."

"I already got one open," I said. "Let's get away from this fire."

The house was one of those Victorian double parlor layouts. With the sliding double doors between them open, the two rooms were like one big room. We went back into the first parlor where I'd thrown the chair through the French window, Uncle Roddy unbuttoning the jacket of his gray flannel suit and loosening his tie. He sat in one of the wing chairs.

"The guy must be one of Cotton's friends. No burglar takes time to light a fire." He was breathing hard.

"That's possible," I agreed. I pushed the curtain back so he could get some air.

"I notice the Diamond broad qualified her statement about not seein' the guy *here* before. That don't mean she hasn't seen him somewhere else."

"That's possible." I picked up the iron chair, and went through the broken window to put it back on the porch. Through the bushes I could see the patrol car leaving.

"Sure she has," he called to me. "I assume she's been tailing Cotton for the past couple of weeks."

"That's possible, too," I said, coming back in. I started to push the other wing chair back to where it had been before I'd charged through the window.

"'That's possible,'" he bellowed. "'That's possible.' 'I'm not free to tell you that,'" mimicking a little girl and screwing up his face trying to look sweet. "What the hell is going on here, Neal? Are you gonna sit down and talk to me or clean house the rest of the night?" His face was turning purple.

I sat down fast. "Calm down, Uncle Roddy. Of course I'm going to talk to you."

Fonte came in through the front door with a smirk on his face.

"What?" Uncle Roddy demanded. "You back from Touro already? You got a winged chariot or somethin'?"

"I had Clift and Gaudet take her over," Fonte said. "I figured I would be more help to you here."

This was undoubtedly a veiled reference to what a dangerous character I am. Phil Fonte hasn't liked me much since I knocked his older brother's nose out of joint after school one day. People in this town can't forget something that happened twenty years ago because nothing changes in New Orleans. The same people you went to grammar school with still live down the block from you.

A lot of air was rushing to get through Uncle Roddy's nose. "All right, Fonte. Take a look at the broad's car, will you?"

"Done, Lieutenant. Nothin' unusual."

Uncle Roddy gave up trying to get rid of little Phil. "You were sayin', Neal?"

"I was saying that the way things are shaping up, you're probably right, Lieutenant"—I've been instructed not to be familiar with Uncle Roddy in front of subordinates—"that Lee Diamond was tailing Cotton. Cotton hired me to watch his wife. She got on a plane for Mexico City this evening."

Fonte laughed. "Doesn't this beat everything, Lieutenant? The husband hires a dick and the wife hires a dick. These uptown richies can find the stupidest ways to spend money. Of course, it keeps the private dicks alive. What a scumbag way to make a living," he said to me.

"Fonte," Uncle Roddy said, "how many times have I told you not to antagonize a witness?"

"He didn't see nothin', Lieutenant."

"All right, Fonte. Why'd Cotton put a tail on his wife, Neal?"

"He just said to watch her; he didn't say why. The only thing he specified was that he didn't want his law partners to know what was going on."

"Lawyers," Fonte said. "Never have met one I liked."

Uncle Roddy and I both pretended we didn't hear him.

"Where is Cotton, Neal?"

"I don't know. I came over here to tell him that his wife left the country."

"Was she alone?" Fonte asked.

Uncle Roddy nodded at me, so I said, "Yes."

"Well," Uncle Roddy said, "my guess is it won't matter worth a dime to us once we question Cotton. He'll identify the burn victim, and there'll be a major domestic crisis in the Cotton household. The D.A. won't press charges against the Diamond woman and she won't press charges against the burn victim. We'll be out of it." He meant the cops.

I started to tell him it was possible, but caught myself in time. "I'm sure you're right, Lieutenant."

He stood up and buttoned his jacket. He reminded me of a whale, the way he was dressed in all that gray flannel and blowing air through his nose. The blow this time, though, was amusement, not exasperation. The way you can tell is that his jowls shake and his big belly moves up and down.

"Since you're into cleaning your client's house for him, Neal, we'll leave the window detail to you," he said and then left.

It took me awhile to find everything I needed to board up the window. While I was hammering plywood and securing shutters, I had that uncomfortable feeling that I was being watched. I kept looking up at the windows of the neighbors' houses, but there was no one in any of them. I went back inside and waited until the fire was dead. Cotton still had not shown up, as I'd hoped, so I left him a note that his house had not been burgled, and to call me as soon as he got home, and to talk to me before he talked to the police. Those Good Samaritan acts saved my life.

2

A Drink
with Maurice

The only car from which there was a view of Cotton's front door was a brown Olds station wagon, three or four years old, parked across the street. There were a bunch of grocery bags in the back of it, and as I got closer I could see rolls of toilet paper, a box of Cheerios, a sack of dog food, that kind of stuff in the bags. On the back seat were some toys, on the front seat a box of Handi-Wipes. I looked again at the groceries. There wasn't anything perishable that I could see in any of the bags. And Fonte had said there was nothing unusual. Well, I guess there wasn't if all you thought about was that Lee Diamond is a woman. Uncle Roddy would have taken a second look. And then Uncle Roddy would have laughed at her cover.

I went straight to Touro Infirmary, but she wasn't there; she had never been admitted. I went to the emergency room first, then I double-checked at the front desk. No record at all of a Lee Diamond.

It seemed best to stick close to Cotton's house and hope he came home soon. I could wait at Maurice's.

Maurice and I have been friends since he was on the district attorney's staff, where he started his career, and I was a rookie at the New Orleans Police Department. In the second phase of Maurice's career, he went into private practice, a premeditated

9

choice that was part of Maurice's Big Game Plan. A few years later, I, too, went into private practice, but in no way was this move premeditated. I thought I would be a cop forever, straight on into retirement, just like my father and his father before him. Instead I met Myra Ledet.

A tough, streetwise cop isn't supposed to fall in love with a call girl. Maybe if she'd told me that's what she was I wouldn't have. But, then, a call girl isn't supposed to fall in love with a cop either. Maybe that's why she didn't tell me.

When she finally did, when she couldn't stand any more of the pressure I was putting on her for more time, she cried. I told her it was okay, that she didn't have to do it anymore, live that kind of life. She said she'd thought about it, hard, but she liked the money and the glamour too much to give it up. She went out with some rich, high-powered men. One of them was Salvadore Angelesi, the district attorney of New Orleans, a corrupt power monger, the kind of flashy, egomaniacal politician that makes the whole state of Louisiana stink with rotten politics.

Angry and hurt, I tried to stay away from Myra. It didn't last two weeks; I convinced myself she would change because she loved me.

Two years later Myra was murdered. The only thing left I had to care about was getting Angelesi for killing her. Trying to prove it ruined my career, but the rest of my life was ruined, so what did I care.

Actually, I didn't get thrown off the police force. I left before they told me I had to, and let Maurice talk me into becoming an investigator. He gave me my first case.

Maurice lives in the Garden District, where I'd just come from and where Richard Cotton lives. Maurice's house is in the next block up toward St. Charles Avenue, so I passed Cotton's to see if he'd gotten home, but his car still wasn't in the driveway. The brown Olds wasn't parked out in front of his house either. There was something about this that didn't sit quite right. You see, Touro Infirmary is at most a five-minute drive from Cotton's house. A good hour and a half must have elapsed between the time patrolmen Clift and Gaudet would have dropped Lee Diamond off at the hospital, and the time I finished boarding up the window and watching the fire die. If she hadn't gone into the emergency room for treatment, then . . . I could feel those eyes on me all over again.

It was getting late, but I wasn't worried about waking Maurice. He's a real genius type, never sleeping, forgetting to eat, always working, and he doesn't give a thought to time unless he has to be in court or has an appointment, in which case he is scrupulously punctual.

Maurice answered the door, dressed, as usual, in a black three-piece Western-cut suit and black cowboy boots. Maurice is in no way your average lawyer. In this town, any other lawyer who dressed like that would be dismissed as weird. But Maurice is so smart he's just eccentric.

I told him what had been going on as we walked through the house to what used to be a den but now looks like a law office, the only setting other than a courtroom in which Maurice is comfortable. The rest of the house is like a museum; nothing has been changed since his parents died.

Maurice sat behind his desk in the law office away from the law office, and looked at me through the thick lenses of his glasses, which never sit perfectly straight on his face. Even though they're heavy black horn-rims, they made him wide-eyed and boyish—a whiz kid. But when he talked he sounded anything but boyish. His voice belongs in a courtroom—he has trouble keeping it down.

"So she knocked him in the fireplace and left him there?" he asked. I might have been on the witness stand.

"She said he tried to kill her with the poker. She took a severe blow on the neck."

"Who is this woman?"

"Her name is Lee Diamond." The eyes really did get wide. "You know her?"

"I went to law school with her."

"I thought she was an investigator."

He nodded. "She dropped out after her second year. She does

mostly paralegal-type work, research, questioning of witnesses, photography; she's very good at it. I've hired her a couple of times, but the last time I called her, she turned me down, so I assume she keeps busy. She could sue Richard Cotton, you know. So could the man who burned in the fireplace."

"Well, it would be good if I could find Richard to tell him what happened in his house tonight."

"He's probably across the lake."

"What's across the lake?" I asked.

"The Colonel's estate," Maurice said.

Colonel Cotton, Richard's deceased father, was not a military man, but he went around in military-type suits—epaulets, lots of gold buttons, an American flag stickpin always in his lapel. He was the founder of the Cotton National Bank, an institution where the way you are treated has a lot more to do with who you know and what your name is rather than how much money you have, although if you know the right people, you usually have plenty enough money. A bank like this can thrive in a class-conscious city like New Orleans. Like the Cottons themselves, it has snob appeal.

"It's an old plantation home on the Bogue Falaya," Maurice said, "right in the heart of Covington, but once you're on the grounds, it feels like it's miles away from anything. Richard used to spend a lot of time over there."

"Hm. Seems like he would have given me a number if he'd planned to be across the lake for any length of time."

"With the rumors flying the way they are," Maurice said with that in-the-know nonchalance of his, "he probably went over there to escape a lot of questions."

"What rumors?" I demanded. It's true that Maurice is a veritable font of information, but when he seems to have more information at his command about my client than I do, it makes me irritable.

"Where have you been, Neal?"

"Where have I been? I've been tailing his wife from stores to restaurants to beauty parlors and back to stores. What rumors are you talking about?"

"Word's been out for the past few days that Cotton's going to give Callahan a run for his money in this year's election."

Clarence "Chance" Callahan was the district attorney of New Orleans. In the three years since he'd been elected he'd been at the center of a lot of controversy, most of which had to do with blacks and the police. There had been several incidents of alleged police brutality and violation of civil rights, standard fare for New Orleans, but when Callahan had not immediately prosecuted several police officers for murder after four blacks were gunned down by the officers in a housing project, the black community had been outraged. The police had gone into the project to question suspects about a cop murder that had happened a few days before, and they claimed that they'd shot the suspects in self-defense. There were plenty of questionable circumstances, however, like the fact that two raids occurred simultaneously on different sides of the project, and in both raids a single suspect had decided to draw a gun against four or five cops; and in an earlier, separate case of a black man who had been shot, a knife.

Of course, the cops had on their side the fact that none of these suspects were models of upstanding citizenship, a career criminal and drug dealer among them. There was some appeasement while a grand jury investigated the shootings, but when it came back saying there was not enough evidence to bring the policemen to trial, the entire city was paralyzed with fear of race riots. A lot of the blame for this menace was put on Callahan by the whites, who were demanding more and better police protection, as well as by the blacks, since it's pretty well known that if a powerful district attorney wants to prosecute, he can usually get a grand jury to go along with him.

There had been no riots, but for a long time blacks had picketed outside City Hall and Callahan's office with signs reading, WE HAVE NO CHANCE WITH CALLAHAN. The city was calmer now, but the matter was far from settled and didn't look as if it would be before the election.

"Can you believe this?" I asked Maurice. "I've talked to the man almost every day for the past two weeks and he's failed to tell me he wants to run for district attorney."

"Look at it this way—you wouldn't be in business if people are discreet when they're supposed to be or talk when they have something to say."

"You lawyers have great powers of rationalization," I said. "I guess Richard figures I don't need to know his political ambitions in order to tail his wife. I guess he's right."

"He's going to be very unhappy about what happened at his house tonight. An accident like that shouldn't happen to a man with political ambitions."

"He's also going to be very unhappy to find out his wife's got a tail on him." I rubbed a hand down over my face. "I could use a drink, Maurice."

Maurice went out to the kitchen, but I could hear the perfect courtroom voice without any trouble. "What's he doing hiring a shadow for his old lady at a time like this? He needs to clean up his act."

I wish Maurice wouldn't try to use slang or talk like a regular person—it doesn't sound right on him. His voice resounds too much; his elocution is too good for slang. He almost sounds like a foreigner when he says things like "clean up his act" or calls someone's wife his "old lady."

"I hate to say it, Neal, but he needs to get rid of you, reinstate family unity, and work on presenting an image as the strong arm of the law instead of rich Southern white boy." Ah, that was more like it. "No Scotch."

"Bourbon, then."

"I'm surprised Lee Diamond took on divorce work, if that's what she's doing."

"You're just saying that because she turned you down. Paula Cotton probably pays her better than you do."

There was silence in the kitchen. "Just kidding, Maurice." Sometimes he doesn't pick up on my more subtle jokes.

"Um, no bourbon, Neal."

"What do you have?"

I could hear bottles rattling. "Grenadine, vermouth and rum."

"Rum and soda."

I heard cabinet doors banging. He was probably looking for a jigger. Or maybe a clean glass.

He walked into the room and said, "She should have been a lawyer."

I clutched at my chest. "Okay, okay," I said. "You got me where it hurts."

"I meant nothing against your profession, Neal." Maurice knows what a sensitive guy I am. "She has something better than great powers of rationalization."

"What's that?"

"Great powers of intimidation, and"—he jiggled his brows behind his slightly lopsided glasses—"an innate sense of when to leave your scruples at home." He hummed a small sigh. "She would have made a great trial lawyer." He handed me a suspicious-looking drink.

"What's this?"

"Rum and grapefruit juice. I seem to be out of everything."

Well, you can't expect a genius to remember to go to the store if he can't remember to eat.

I backtracked to Richard Cotton's house one more time before heading down St. Charles Avenue to the Euclid Apartments where I live. Cotton still wasn't home and I didn't want to be.

The Euclid was a nice place when I moved in four years ago, but I wouldn't call it that anymore. I'll give you some examples: I parked in the parking garage, as usual, and when I got out of my car, the first thing I saw was that someone had thrown up in the slot next to mine. Inside, the lobby was dim because several bulbs had burned out and no one had bothered to replace them. It was bright enough, though, that I could see that the same leftover drinks in plastic cups were still sitting where they'd been discarded the weekend before, on the furniture, one in a plant, another on the floor by the elevators. One of the elevators was broken and had been for almost two weeks. I stood and watched the other one go back and forth between the fourth and fifth floors, and finally hiked up to my apartment on the sixth.

My apartment was freezing. The heating unit in it had been working off and on, mostly off, for the entire month of December and into January, the coldest, wettest and dreariest month of the winter in New Orleans. It's the kind of cold that goes right through you, gets in your bones and makes them feel like pieces of ice trying to bend. Mine felt that way now. Some of the residents had told me they'd heard the Euclid was going condo. They were upset about it. Not me. I wished it would. Then I would have the motivation to move.

I took a hot shower, fixed a hot toddy, and crawled under the covers with the phone books. I looked up detectives in the Yellow Pages. My small ad was there, but she didn't have any listing at all. She was in the white pages—Lee Diamond, 910 Dumaine. The French Quarter. It wasn't even in boldface. Yes, indeed, she must keep busy, and she must be very particular about the work she took. Probably about her clients, too.

I went to sleep thinking about her, the soft brown hair I'd pushed aside to put the ice pack on her neck, those yellow eyes in the firelight, her voice when she thanked me, her slightly crooked teeth, but it was the burned man I dreamed about.

3

Colonel Cotton's Estate

At eight o'clock the next morning, I still hadn't heard from my client. There was no answer when I called his house. At nine o'clock his office told me that he wasn't expected all day. When I asked where he was, the woman said she didn't know, which I took to mean she wouldn't tell me. I left my name and office number and said I needed to talk to him. I hesitated to say it was urgent, not after the way he'd told me he didn't want his law partners to know he'd hired a private investigator for work outside the firm. I tried Covington directory assistance, but the number was unpublished. I called Maurice. He told me that anyone in Covington could direct me to Colonel Cotton's estate. By nine-fifteen, I was on my way across Lake Pontchartrain.

The weather was foul. When I got to the causeway that goes across the lake, the fog was just beginning to lift enough that the bridge police were letting a few cars at a time start the twenty-four-mile trek. It was drizzling, one of those constant drizzles that never gets any heavier but doesn't let up all day either. By the time it was my turn to cross, visibility was still low, so it was a slow crawl across the long bridge with nothing to look at but the choppy brown water of the lake. It looked like Mississippi River water.

I drove into the thriving little town of Covington, crossing the Bogue Falaya River to get to the downtown area. When I was a kid

17

my family used to vacation at some cabins on the Bogue Falaya that were right down a hill from the main drag through town. In my kid's mind, we were completely surrounded by woods for miles, although I do remember going to a movie theater to see a Three Stooges movie a couple of times. Since I'd seen the movie twice, I thought it was the only movie shown at that theater, and the next few times we came back to Covington, I was disappointed and angry that I couldn't see Larry, Curly and Moe. I remember the old man really getting a kick out of it, and that made me even madder.

The sign for the cabins was all that was left. It stood to the side of the bridge across the river, but rivulets of rust and peeling paint made it hard to read the name anymore. I got past the sign and my childhood memories; the town of Covington has a new face on it, the face of prosperity. The two major causes of this change are crime and the high price of real estate in New Orleans. People have been moving across the lake in droves for the past few years so they can get a bigger piece of land with a bigger house on it for less money and not be in a marginal neighborhood or have one a block away. They say they're moving to the country, to Life Beyond the Burglar Alarm, but with subdivisions, shopping centers and fast food places popping up like mad, it's not the country anymore.

The first person I asked told me exactly how to get to the Cotton estate. When Maurice said it was in the heart of town, he hadn't exaggerated. It was through some back streets only a few blocks from the gas station downtown where I'd stopped for directions, but when I turned in to the shelled driveway I was in another world. Through the rain and mist I could see a tennis court equipped with night lights and a small viewing stand. Beyond that was a swimming pool flanked by a West Indies–type structure that was too big to be just a changing area. Thick foliage surrounded the grounds and made it private. A high wall of bamboo blocked any view of the tennis court from the front, and ran down one side of the drive. Behind the pool, fencing in that side of the property, were the tallest, thickest camellia bushes I've ever seen. They were in bloom and I could see dots of red for a long way in the thinning fog.

I went around a curve and there was the plantation, big and white and unexpected, so suddenly was it in front of me. To my left the ground sloped down to a small lagoon. To the right was another structure, a guest house maybe, or the servants' quarters. Another shelled road curved up around it. I pulled the car to the top of the horseshoe driveway in front of the mansion.

At ground level, an open brick veranda ran around the house. Above, on the second story, was another railed veranda. Fog was clinging to the house in pearly-white patches that were moving gradually toward the roofline, disembodied idle drifters that made the house seem dead. I went up the wide wood steps to the leaded glass doors at the top and rang the bell.

I didn't really expect an answer, since my car was the only one around, but through the glass I could see a figure coming toward me.

He was a young black man, in his mid to late twenties, and while I told him my name and that I was looking for Mr. Cotton, he smiled pleasantly, perhaps a bit spacily, at me. He was tall and slim and very well turned out in a white silk shirt and sharply creased jeans. His skin was smooth, a rich and unblemished *café au lait* color. His bright smile, his jaunty way of holding himself seemed to me to have something of the Caribbean in it, but maybe I just thought that because the pool house reminded me of the West Indies. He told me Cotton wasn't there.

"Mind if I come in and use the phone?" I asked.

"Sure, boss," he said, "you come in. You come in out of this bad weather." He didn't look, act or sound like any servant I'd ever seen before, in spite of what he said. He enunciated clearly, with just a hint of a black dialect, his speech soft, rounded, rhythmic. He stepped back, a graceful, dancerlike movement.

I entered the wide center hallway with its dark, gleaming floors. He walked with me to the end, where there was a phone on a small table, and then he disappeared discreetly into another room. I used my credit card number and called my answering service.

They kept me on hold much longer than they should have to see if I had any messages. As I waited, I noticed a few things, like the fact that the place on the phone where there should have been a number was blank, that outside the French doors I was standing in front of there was a two-car garage that was all closed up, and that I was catching a whiff of a smell, smoky, sweet, a little medicinal, but vague, nothing that was burning now. Then it was gone and I wasn't sure I'd smelled it. The answering service came back on and told me Lieutenant Rankin had called.

I waited for about ten seconds before I started toward the front door. From a room on the opposite side of the hallway than the one he'd gone into, the black man reappeared. His step, even on those hardwood floors, was light, almost without sound.

"What's your name?" I asked.

"Quiro." He gave it a Spanish flavor—the first syllable sounding like "key," a bit of roll on the "r," his heels coming together as he said it.

"What's your status around here, Quiro?"

"I look after the house, the grounds." He gestured toward outside.

"Must keep you busy."

"Not on a day like today." He was still smiling, not minding my inquisitiveness at all.

"Do you know how I can reach Mr. Cotton?"

"He keeps very busy all the time, boss." Seemed to me that Quiro had been well trained to be polite, show no curiosity, and offer no information.

"I need to talk to him, Quiro."

"Lots of people need to talk to him, boss, but I'll tell him for you." There was some indication that he was doing me a favor, but not that he was pointedly telling me so. He opened the door.

"You do that," I said, and ducked back out into the rain.

4

The Lure
of the Diamond

I drove back to town and went up to my office in the Père Marquette, a central business district office building owned by the Jesuits. My office decor used to be a style best described as seedy—drab, bare floor, odd pieces of used furniture—but my sister redecorated it for me after a madman who thought I was fooling around with his girlfriend destroyed almost everything in it. That had happened the summer before, in August, but I didn't fully appreciate my sister's effort to make the place warm and comfortable until the weather got so nasty. On a day like today it looked pretty good, a much better place to be than the Euclid. I looked at the long sofa across from my desk and thought I'd just stay here until the heating unit got fixed at the apartment, but I knew that even some warmth wouldn't make the Euclid feel like home. I wondered if I was turning into a lone creature like Maurice, who was only at home in his office, only happy while he was working, and so worked all the time. As much as I like and admire Maurice, I didn't want that to happen to me.

I returned Uncle Roddy's call, but he was out, so I got to work completing a report on a personal injury case for Maurice, probably the one Lee Diamond had turned down. There was more left to do than I'd thought, and I didn't finish until late in the afternoon. I thought about calling Lee Diamond, but I was stiff

21

from all the sitting I'd been doing. I put on my raincoat and walked across Canal Street through the French Quarter to Dumaine Street.

Number 910 was a Spanish structure, smooth terra-cotta stucco with a gateway entrance to the side. There was a row of mailboxes. Hers was the last one. I rang the bell under it and identified myself over an intercom. After being buzzed in, I walked down an alleyway to a courtyard with a small fountain, a lot of banana trees, a patio table and some chairs. Her apartment was in the two-story back part of the building that faced the courtyard, which was once the slave quarters. It was attached to the main building upstairs by a balcony, downstairs by a walkway, so it was apart and private. She leaned in the downstairs doorway, her arms folded across a camel-colored dress, a soft, sort of hairy-looking dress that was really just a long, close-fitting sweater. It had another one of those high cowl necklines, but below that I could see very clearly what hadn't been so well defined the night before. Dressed like this, with brown high heels, a green tint to the glasses she was wearing, and more curl to the hair around her face, she seemed very different, like another person, sophisticated, elegant. She didn't look at all as quick and strong as I knew she was, or as if she'd ever be caught dead dressed like she'd been the night before. Those glamorous, movie-version cat burglars came to mind.

She brought me into her office, and sat behind her desk rather carefully.

"How's your neck?" I asked.

"Hurting," she said simply, not asking for sympathy.

"Why didn't you go get it looked at?"

"Because they would have looked at it, then poked at it, then x-rayed it, then told me to do what I could have been at home doing two hours earlier."

She smiled when I did. I watched the way her upper lip bowed just a bit, lifting slightly over her overlapping front teeth, curving down as she smiled to create distinct laugh lines at the sides of her mouth. I was fascinated by what those crooked teeth did for her lips.

"What can I do for you, Mr. Rafferty?"

"My name is Neal," I said. "You can tell me where Richard Cotton is."

"I don't know," she said.

Here was something else about her: When she'd smiled at me moments before, her face had lit up with warmth and friendliness, maybe even more—sharing a joke with an intimate; now when she said, "I don't know," it could have meant something or it could have meant nothing. I couldn't hear any ambiguity in her tone, I couldn't read the expression on her face. I wished she'd take those glasses off.

I shook a cigarette out of a pack and offered it to her.

"No thank you." She opened a desk drawer, took out an ashtray, and slid it toward me. I watched for some sign of disapproval that I smoked, but, again, there was nothing.

"I'll bet I could bargain with you if you didn't already know where your client is," I said as tonelessly as I could, looking at her over the flame I held to my cigarette. I'm cool as hell when the occasion calls for it.

Her eyes didn't leave me until she started laughing. She threw her head back just a little too far and winced with pain, but still she kept on laughing. Actually, the situation was pretty ludicrous.

"No, Neal," she said finally. "We still couldn't bargain—I really don't know where your client is. I lost him around midday yesterday and never did find him. That's why I was out in front of his house last night."

"Well, if you think I'm embarrassed because I can't find my client," I said, "forget it." She laughed again. "The burned man, Lee—did you ever see him with Cotton?"

"No." There it was, that same inscrutability, the same possibility that she was somehow outside the truth, stretching it or testing it—or lying. I hated to admit it to myself because I liked her, but I thought she was lying.

Perhaps my question had been too specific. "Do you know of any connection he has to Cotton?"

"I know what you know, that he had a way into Cotton's house."

The way she said it, I believed her now, and my own sudden involuntary change in the way I was thinking confused me. If only I could see her eyes better . . .

"Are you going to press charges against him?" I asked.

"So no one has told you," she answered quietly. "He died this morning."

"I guess that's why Uncle Roddy called," I murmured.

"Who's Uncle Roddy?" she asked, but I didn't answer her. I was looking at her and thinking that she had stood there watching him burn up in the fireplace. "Neal?" she was saying. "Who is Uncle Roddy?"

"Oh. Lieutenant Rankin. We've been missing each other today." I think that's what I said, anyway. I was feeling off balance, the way you get when there's something going on that you don't understand and no one is going to explain it to you. "Did they identify him?"

"By his fingerprints. His name was Christopher Raven. They ran a rap sheet—drug possession seven years ago, suspended sentence. A year later he was picked up again for dealing. They cut a deal with him down in narcotics and put him back on the street."

Christopher Raven had become what is known as a rat, an informant. I asked her if she knew who the cop was he'd ratted for. These vice cops and their rats become like family to each other. The cop would know just about everything there was to know about Raven—how he got his money, what kind of drugs he used, if he was trustworthy, if he was a coward, who else his old lady slept with—and he would have used it to put the heat on Raven if he got uncooperative. For Raven's trouble he would get enough drugs to keep him dependent. Most of the rats had to turn to a life of crime to get the money they needed to live. They also had to make sure they had some information, even if they made it up, so they could get their drugs. The informant system of fighting crimes is ugly, breeding more crime. The average cop doesn't have the stomach for vice.

The cop was no one I knew, someone named Delahoussaye.

She'd talked to him that morning while she was downtown to see Uncle Roddy. Delahoussaye told her Raven never had given him much he could use, and then he decided he wanted to go straight, and got on a methadone program. He got cut loose and Delahoussaye hadn't seen him for about two years. He said Raven had no known relatives, no current address and was bisexual. He had a half ounce of cocaine on him, some heroin, and track marks on his arms and legs. The "fit" was tied to his calf, which was where he always wore it, Delahoussaye told her. The "fit," the outfit, is the drugs and all the drug paraphernalia—needle, spoon, something to tie off with.

She gave me the information very matter-of-factly. I thanked her, told her she'd saved me some legwork.

"Lieutenant Rankin," she asked, "he's your uncle?"

I was too curious to leave her yet, but I wanted out of her territory, away from the white walls, the shelves of books that went all the way up to the ceiling, away from having to look at the fireplace that was behind her. I wanted her desk from in between us. "Uh, Lee, would you like to go get a drink with me? I'll tell you all about him."

We went into the outer reception area where my raincoat, hanging from a coatrack, was still dripping. There was a white desk with a typewriter on it, a sleek sofa and a glass coffee table. Through another doorway I could see a refrigerator. A spiral staircase was off in a corner.

"What's upstairs?" I asked.

"Books, files and a sofa bed." She took a black hooded cloak out of a closet, and before I could help her, she had it around her and was buttoning it at the neck.

The rain had stopped, but it was still misty and it felt as if it was getting colder. Lee pulled the hood up over her head, and we went through the alleyway to Dumaine Street. I stopped out front, trying to decide which way to go.

"I don't drink," Lee told me, so we walked over to The Coffee Pot, a small restaurant on St. Peter.

Over my drink and her espresso, I told her about Uncle Roddy and the old man, some things about the Irish Channel where I grew up, and that I had quit the New Orleans Police Department to become a private investigator. Talking to her seemed to open up my memory, especially when I was telling her what it was like to grow up in the Channel, but when it came to my resignation from the NOPD, I was very selective. I didn't tell her about Angelesi or Myra Ledet, or any of the trouble all that had caused me.

I could tell by the way she talked that she wasn't from New Orleans, although she said it was the first place she'd been long enough to say she was from and call home. Her father had been an officer in the Marines, and they'd lived everywhere from North Carolina and Virginia to San Diego, coming to New Orleans when Lee was old enough to think about college. That was how she ended up going to law school at Tulane University.

I let her know that Maurice had told me a few things about her, like she'd dropped out of school. "How'd you get in this racket?" I asked.

One elbow on the table, she rested her chin in her cupped hand. "There was a man, a detective." She smiled slightly. "I worked for him one summer. That was the end of school."

I wanted to ask her if she was sorry she'd left Tulane for him, if she'd ever thought of going back. I wanted to ask her a lot of things, but she sat back, like she was finished talking about those things now, and, anyway, I certainly didn't want her to get curious about my origins in this business. I thought she looked a little dreamy, but who could tell.

"It's nighttime," I said. "Why don't you put your sunglasses away?"

"Because they look a lot better than this." She took the glasses off, and pushed her hair back, away from her left temple. She'd taken a blow on her head, right above the temple, when the man had jumped her, and it had caused her eyelid and the area around the corner of her eye to turn purplish and black. The place on her head was raised. It looked nasty, and it looked dangerous.

I reached across the table to put my hand up to it, but she

flinched away, a reflex reaction. I put my hand down. She put her glasses back on.

"I really think you ought to have someone look at that," I said.

"I saw a doctor today. There's not too much brain damage, not from being hit, anyway."

This is what I mean about the way she could get you to react to her: Suddenly I wasn't so off balance; I didn't feel so confused. Once I thought I understood that she was having some feelings about what had happened last night that I could identify with, the first thing about her that really got to me, I think, was her crooked teeth. God, they were sexy.

"Would you like to have dinner here," I asked her, "or go someplace else?"

"I've got to go home, Neal. I don't think I can sit up much longer."

It's hard to get a check and get out of The Coffee Pot quickly, but I managed. She didn't live above her office as I'd supposed, but had an apartment uptown on Exposition Boulevard. Exposition Boulevard isn't a street; it's a sidewalk on the edge of Audubon Park. When you live on Exposition Boulevard, Audubon Park is your front yard. I walked with her to the lot where she kept her car. It wasn't the brown Olds, but an all-black Mustang convertible. I didn't say anything about the Olds or the groceries. She offered me a ride, but I told her I didn't know where I was going yet. I watched her pull out and speed off so she could make it across Rampart Street before the light turned red.

I would have felt lonely walking through the French Quarter with no place to go and nothing in particular to do except that right before she drove off, she told me she'd have dinner with me the next night.

5

Simpático

If you think the next thing I'm going to tell you is that my client turned up dead, you're wrong. He turned up three days later with a tan. He'd been in Acapulco with his wife.

Phil Fonte got to Richard before Richard got to me the night he returned, and, on Rankin's orders, gave him a ride downtown, but Richard said he'd never heard of Christopher Raven nor, after looking at his mug shots, could he recall ever having seen him. We met in his office early the next morning and were talking about why he'd gone to Mexico so suddenly.

"Paula called me and told me she was going to Acapulco to think things over," he said. "We've been having some trouble for a while." He shifted in his chair, more uncomfortable with what he was telling me than with the way he was sitting.

Discomfort did not look good on Richard Cotton. He had that blond all-American kind of good looks. With his tan he could have been a surfer, except that the beachboy image was tempered by his slim-faced intelligence, his experienced blue eyes, and a straight lean body that looked best in a continental-cut suit. He was supposed to exude self-confidence, not look uncomfortable.

"People don't usually call in a private detective unless there's trouble, Richard." I wanted to put him at ease. I liked Richard Cotton. He and I were *simpático*, as they say. He was a few years younger than I am, but he'd been around as a prosecutor during

Angelesi's heyday, and he knew more than the average person
about my involvement in Angelesi's fall. But we didn't talk too
much about each other's personal lives. Not usually. We were just
simpático.

He said, "I know, but it probably isn't what you're thinking.
Paula's been acting strange lately, remote. I thought maybe she
was seeing another man."

"That's about what I was thinking," I told him. "After all,
suspicion of adultery is the number one reason people hire
detectives to follow their spouses. You want a divorce?"

"No. I don't want a divorce." He was very emphatic. "There's
never been a divorce in my family. God, my father would flip in
his grave."

So what? I thought, but that was just sour grapes. I knew
Richard had practically hero-worshiped his father—still did—and
I guess I was envious. The Colonel had wanted Richard to go into
the banking business, but when Richard told him he wanted to
take a lowly job as a prosecutor, the Colonel had backed him all
the way. At one time I'd thought my old man and I were tight
enough that I could tell him I wanted to be a private cop and he
would have given me his blessings. I also thought I could tell him
Myra was a call girl. But after she died, and I started pointing the
finger at Angelesi, all he could ask me was why Angelesi would
bother to kill the likes of Myra? Mostly what it was, he couldn't
take the idea that I wasn't going to be a cop anymore.

"Okay, you don't want a divorce, but I'm tailing Paula anyway."

Richard said, "Yes, I've decided to run against Callahan next
fall."

"Are we having the same conversation?" I asked. "Maybe I'm
being dense. Are you telling me that I've been following Paula
because you want to run for D.A.?"

He was moving around in his chair again, not meeting my eyes.
"I was jealous, too."

Like heck he was. He sat forward. "Look, if she's seeing another
man, it's my own fault. Paula wants to have children, and I'm not
sure I do—I mean, I want to eventually, just not yet."

"But she's not seeing another man, Richard. She went to Acapulco with you, right?"

"Yes. Well, I followed her down there."

"I know."

It was supposed to get a laugh, but he just got more fidgety. "When she called me the other day and said she was going to think things over, I knew that if I let her go alone, it was the end of our marriage. I really don't want that to happen, but between the law practice and planning campaign strategy, I haven't had any time for her. I'm embarrassed to tell you this—it was truly thoughtless—but she found out I was going to run for D.A. when I announced it at a dinner party we had one night. Anyway, I told her to go on to Mexico City, and that after I'd taken care of a few things I'd fly down in our plane and we'd go to Acapulco together. We talked everything over. She's with me all the way on the D.A.'s race. And she's trying to get pregnant."

Well, I didn't have to be psychic to get the feeling that there were plenty of problems with Richard and Paula's marriage, and who was running around on who probably wasn't the biggest one. More like a symptom of the disease. It was a shame. He had looks and money, a good name, a gorgeous wife, he was ambitious, and he was smart. He probably had inherited enough money that he would never have to work again. Instead, he'd worked hard, first as a prosecutor, then, sometime around when Callahan took over, he'd struck out on his own, started all over, and was building a successful law firm. The reputation he had as a lawyer was well deserved. He'd achieved a lot for his age, but from the look he had on his handsome face now, I wouldn't have given a dime that any of it had made him happy. I also wouldn't have given a dime that his thoughts at the moment had anything to do with his marital problems.

It wasn't my business, but for the first time since I'd known Richard Cotton, I was seeing him as a troubled man. "So you wanted to make sure Paula wasn't running around on you. You want to be a squeaky-clean politician, a family man. I don't get it.

You're not running for President. I mean, this is New Orleans, Richard. You can hardly live here and be clean."

He simply wasn't reacting to my jokes today. "I'm talking about a very dirty campaign, Neal. If you knew even some of the things I know about Chance Callahan, you'd understand."

"Like what?"

"Like some big-time drug and vice operations going on in this town and Callahan's getting rich off them."

"The same stuff Angelesi was into?"

Now he laughed. "Oh, sure, there're the bribes, the extortion, the blackmail, all the petty racketeering. You know as well as I do that Callahan was spoonfed his experience by Angelesi, but he's gone on to things that Angelesi wouldn't have even thought about, much bigger things."

"And you are talking Big Trouble, Richard."

He shook his head. "I don't want him to be able to fling one little speck of dirt at me."

"There's always a little speck of dirt. For instance, what happened at your house the other night would qualify as being pretty unsavory." I told him what I'd found out about Raven from Lee Diamond. He turned a little pale under that Acapulco tan. "If you're planning on making any accusations, I'd think twice."

Then he got angry. "If Callahan was doing his job right, this town wouldn't be on the top ten list for crime in the country. I was just another victim. People all over uptown are screaming for better police protection."

"Oh, come on. That's great political rhetoric, but you don't have to impress me. *White* people all over uptown have been screaming for protection against blacks ever since the project killings. That man in your house wasn't black, not before he fell into the fireplace, anyway. What are you going to say, that Christopher Raven was breaking and entering to support his drug habit?"

"Well, what the hell else was he doing?"

"I don't know, but he didn't break in. Besides, who went to the trouble to make such a nice, cozy fire? No one else was around except Lee Diamond, and she was in her car most of the time."

"Who is this Lee Diamond?" he asked. "What was she doing there?"

"Rankin didn't tell you?" He said Rankin hadn't. "She followed you for two weeks, Richard. Paula hired her."

I think the word I'm looking for now is "blanched"—he blanched under his wonderful tan. I could see he was going to make a fine politician, though, because he recovered fast. All he had to learn how to do was control the blood entering and leaving his face.

"Well, Paula and I have gotten things straight now. All that is over with."

We sat there a few moments not saying anything. I could see he was thinking hard. So was I: Since when did Uncle Roddy get so discreet, I wondered.

"Maybe I can get to the bottom of this thing for you, Richard. Is it possible Quiro made the fire?"

At first I wasn't sure he'd heard me. Then he said, "No. Quiro was across the lake."

"What about keys to your house? Does anyone have any, neighbors, workmen, maids?"

"No. No one except Quiro, and I grew up with him. His mother and father were employed by my father since before I was born. Quiro and I are like brothers. I trust him implicitly."

"But are you sure Quiro didn't let Raven in?"

"He couldn't have. He was across the lake."

"How do you know for sure?" I asked. "You were on your way to Acapulco. I'm not trying to put any blame on Quiro, but if you don't know who Raven was, is it possible that Quiro does?"

"No. The police have already asked him. He'd never seen him."

"Who knew you were going to be out of town?"

He thought about it. "A few people. Not too many. If it will make you feel better, I'll make a list of them."

"Don't do it for me, Richard, do it for yourself. Try in any way you can to help figure out how Raven got into your house and what he was doing there. Could he have overheard you tell anyone you were leaving town, say, in a restaurant? Try to remember anyone who might have had access to your keys—valet parking, a car wash attendant. Or Quiro's keys. What about Paula? Think about it. I'd hate for this incident to ruin anything for you."

"I will, I'll think about it. If I can think of anything at all, I'll let Rankin know. And, thanks, Neal, for everything. Thanks for boarding up the window for me." He stood up. We shook hands.

Maurice was right: He needed to get rid of me and he did.

6

Detective
Without a Case

Later on that night I was discussing Cotton's new persona
with Lee. "He's already acting like a district attorney. He let me
know very neatly that he'd rather work with the police getting a
line on Christopher Raven."

We were in the kitchen at her place. She was fixing us some
kind of Oriental meal. When I tried to repeat the names of the
dishes, she laughed and said it sounded like a bad imitation of
baby talk. There were little bowls of chopped vegetables, fish and
shrimp on the counter. She'd put on the rice, and was taking a
large wok out of one of the cabinets.

Lee's apartment reflected her fascination with the Orient. It was
done in the Japanese style, sparsely furnished, everything low to
the floor. A lot of the things had been sent to her by her father
when he was on a tour of duty in the Far East. The only chair in
the place was one at a small desk in the living room. When we
ate, we sat on cushions around a black-lacquered table. The sofa
was a folded futon. The first night I spent with her, I told her it
was going to be hard for me to get used to these sitting positions—
my knees somehow didn't feel right being so close to my chin. She
told me I'd get used to it if I wanted to. In the bedroom was
another futon, large and unfolded. She told me the next morning
that I had a great future with futons.

When I wasn't with Lee, I was at the office. The only time I'd been home during those days was to get some clothes. The Euclid was fading from my memory, which felt good. I hadn't even bothered to make my usual daily complaint about the heat, or lack of it. For all I knew it was fixed. I really didn't care.

Lee oiled the wok. "If he wants to be the next D.A.," she said about Richard, "he'll do well to make friends with the police."

"I wish him all the luck in the world with Roderick Rankin," I said.

Lee turned away from her culinary creation long enough to ask, "Do I detect some bitterness toward Richard Cotton that he took you off this case?"

"What makes you think that?"

"You're a friend of his, aren't you? He did confide in you, didn't he?"

"So that makes me bitter?" I never did like that word unless it was plural and went into a mixed drink.

"Okay, Neal, you're not bitter. I sense that something about what he said to you didn't go down quite right. Or maybe you didn't feel he was being completely straight with you. I don't know because I don't know exactly what he said. Would mixed emotions be a better choice of words?"

Actually, she was getting pretty close to the truth. There had been something about my conversation with Richard that hadn't gone down right, but I wasn't sure what it was. I said, "Let's just say I'm disappointed. This Christopher Raven was the most interesting thing I had going, but Richard wants me out of it, so as far as I'm concerned now, it's the cops' headache. After all, a detective without a client is a detective without a case." Lee was frying the vegetables, taking them one at a time in order of their lineup. "That's not true," I said. "Raven was not the most interesting thing I had going."

I went up behind her and put my arms around her waist. I kissed the side of her neck that wasn't bruised.

She said, "Do you want me to ruin dinner? I'll make you take me to the most expensive restaurant in town if this isn't any good." When I didn't move right away, she said, "Beat it. This kitchen isn't big enough for the two of us." I stood in the doorway and lit a cigarette. She went on. "It's the one thing I don't like about this apartment. I feel like I'm in a matchbox when I'm in here." She paused. "I wouldn't mind an extra room to work out in either." There were weights and other equipment in both the living room and the bedroom. "But it's on the park. And it doesn't flood here."

"That's the *only* good thing I can say about the Euclid," I remarked.

The spring floods in New Orleans occurred regularly each year, and each year they seemed to get worse. In parts of uptown, as well as some suburbs, if you happened to be out when the rains came, you could find yourself waist deep, even chest deep, in water. The problem uptown is caused by the overflow of the Seventeenth Street Canal, which runs through the city all the way out to Lake Pontchartrain. Apparently the pumping station near the end of the canal can't get the water out of the canal and into the lake fast enough. As far as I understood it, this is because of an inadequate number of pumps, the fact that the existing pumps are antiques, and that a place called Bucktown is in the way of the water. Bucktown is between the pumps and the lake, and the people uptown whose houses flood say Bucktown has to go. The fishermen who live on this small waterway and keep their boats there say this is a bunch of bunk.

So far, the area where Lee lived on Audubon Park had never flooded, which was a good thing since she was on the ground floor of a large old house that had been converted into apartments. That was why the kitchen was so small—it was a part of the living room that had been walled in when the house got cut up.

"So what about your client?" I asked.

"Paula Cotton? What about her?"

"Have you talked to her?"

"Sure. This morning." Lee was moving fast now. Everything seemed to be getting ready at once.

"Does she know her husband had her followed?"

She shot a glance at me. "Does her husband know she had *him* followed?"

She handed me a bowl of rice. I put it on the lacquered table and came back to the doorway. "I guess we should be glad we're out of the Cottons' lives. I would hate it if our work caused any conflict between us, and under the circumstances, it might be hard for us not to talk about it."

Lee handed me another dish. "I'm still on retainer, Neal."

That took me aback. I stood there holding one course of the meal, and Lee stood facing me holding the other. "Why?" I asked. "What does she want you to do?"

"Nothing. Yet." She made a motion with her eyes toward the next room. "Come on. Let's eat."

Of course, we did talk about the Cottons some more that night. Lee didn't know why Paula Cotton wanted her on retainer. When she hired Lee initially, she said it was because she thought Richard was fooling around on her. Paula Cotton could afford to keep Lee on retainer indefinitely, and Richard wouldn't necessarily have to know about it. Paula had her own money; she was from a wealthy family in Baton Rouge who had acres and acres, more acres than I knew existed, of soybean fields in northern Louisiana.

The whole thing puzzled me even if I wasn't being paid to be puzzled anymore. I wondered if Paula wanted a divorce in spite of telling Richard she was behind him in the D.A.'s race, in spite of trying to get pregnant.

I also wondered if anyone had ever bothered to question Paula Cotton about Christopher Raven.

7

Breakfast
with the Old Man

When Lee woke up the next morning, she was hurting. The muscles in her neck and shoulder, besides being sore, were cramped and wouldn't relax. Her left arm was shaking. I couldn't help by massaging the muscles because the contusion, though turning yellow and healing, was still too sensitive. Her cooking great Oriental meals and all of our lovemaking during the past few days were, I was afraid, largely at fault. I told her to take a muscle relaxer and stay home. She said most of what she had to do that day could be handled over the phone, but there was some legwork she couldn't put off. I said I'd do it for her. I liked that I could help her out like this.

The fact that we shared the same profession added a dimension to our relationship that I'd never experienced before. The idea that the woman I slept with was also a woman I could work with excited me. Even though I'd spoken of the possibility, I didn't really think that our work would cause a conflict between us. I thought it would make us that much closer, and that somewhere down the line we would work on cases together. I let my imagination take off—I saw us eventually combining our agencies. Would it be Diamond and Rafferty, or Rafferty and Diamond?

I told her I'd either bring dinner to her, or if she felt better take her out, but for the next couple of days I'd leave her alone and stay at the Euclid. When I left she was in the bathtub, chin deep in hot water, the smell of some kind of Chinese incense rapidly filling the bathroom. I got one nice long kiss before I said I had to go or the scent of the stuff would strangle me.

On the way downtown, I dropped in on my parents. It had been about two weeks since I'd seen them. Also, I was hungry, and my mother usually has enough breakfast for a dozen people.

My parents live in the Irish Channel, in the same house they lived in when I was born. The Channel is an old New Orleans neighborhood that stretches from Magazine Street, which used to be the big, busy street through uptown New Orleans before there was a St. Charles Avenue, and goes all the way to the Mississippi River.

It has a bad reputation, and I don't mean bad in its current sense of good. I mean it's tough and dangerous. People don't walk through the Channel at night. They don't even walk through parts of it during the day. But it's full of people who were born there, are proud to be from there, and wouldn't live anywhere else. Like my old man.

But then the Garden District is full of people who have lived there all their lives and wouldn't live in any other part of town, either. But who can blame them? The Garden District is directly on the opposite side of Magazine Street across from the Channel, but the two places are like the flip sides of a coin. And the Channel comes up tails. It doesn't have all the old oak trees, the big, gorgeous houses; in short, the money. It's got something else, though. I guess it's spirit, fighting spirit. To tell you the truth, I'm proud to be from the Channel.

Since I've gotten disgusted with the Euclid, I've thought many times that I'd move back. But something keeps me from doing that. I'm not sure what it is. Maybe it's a sense that now that I've gotten out, I'd better stay out, that if I go back now, I'll never leave again. I'd end up living on the same side of the double that my parents live in after they are gone, with my sister and her family on the other side. I'd be like the old man, like I was living out his life all over again, with his same cop interests, going to the same places he's gone to all his life, seeing the same people day after day, knowing that a different kind of life went on right on the other side of Magazine Street, after a while not caring. Nothing would ever change.

The old man and I have had our ups and downs through the years. During the past few years, it's been mostly downs. Just when I think he's going to get over the fact that I had to resign from the NOPD, something will happen to get him all riled up again. But this morning I could tell he was glad to see me: He actually got up from the kitchen table and poured me a cup of coffee. He must have told me to sit down three times, and when I did, he threw the early morning edition of the *Times-Picayune* on the table in front of me.

Meanwhile, my mother was bustling around the kitchen cleaning up and telling me to help myself to what was left over from breakfast. She was in a hurry because she was going to the doctor with my sister, who was seven months' pregnant. Reenie was having pains and bleeding a little, and Ma was afraid that the baby would be premature or that Reenie would miscarry. While she was telling me this, the old man was telling me what it was he wanted me to read on the front page of the newspaper. They were both talking to me like the other one wasn't there. It was when Ma started going on about how Reenie had waited too long to have another child and that she was getting too old to be having babies that the old man got aggravated.

"Maureen's gonna be just fine, Mama," he said. "The baby is gonna be fine. Stop worryin' and hurry up and get over there."

"But there's always so much to do," Ma said, and put more dirty dishes down in the suds.

"Go on, go on." He was close to yelling now. Then he said, more calmly, "Go on. I'll finish cleanin' up."

It was a first, and it almost bowled me over. Ma turned around so he could see the look of disbelief on her face, but he had gotten up to get himself another cup. She gave me one of her "Blessed

Mother" looks, eyes heavenward, and said, "Okay, John." She dried her hands, and began gathering up her things.

"Bye, darlin'," she said to me and kissed me on the forehead, then dashed through the house to the front door.

After the door closed, he said, "I think Maureen has babies so your mother will take over next door as well as here. Women." But he wasn't really that disgusted. He put his finger on the article he was so interested in.

The whole time I was reading he talked. He said that between the project killings and this latest episode, Chance Callahan had himself between a rock and a hard place with the blacks, that he'd better do something to appease them since this was election year, that the media was really getting on Callahan now and asking some pretty tough questions. The old man is not a Callahan fan, but, then, he never likes any politician. What he likes is the political dirt. He and Uncle Roddy can sit around for hours laughing about it all, making fun of the politicos. They act like they have the inside track, but it's all just talk. Neither one of them would ever try to buck a powerful New Orleans politician. That's why they thought I was so crazy when I accused Angelesi of murdering Myra.

I read the article rather sketchily because of the distraction. I got the basics, which were that the previous evening, a white policeman had gunned down a black youth who was out riding a motorcycle with a friend. The friend, who wasn't hurt, claimed that the two of them were on their way to another friend's house, and that they were not speeding or breaking any laws, when the police car was suddenly behind them, signaling for them to pull over. They were getting off the motorcycle, the friend said, and the next thing he knew there was a gunshot, and his buddy was on the ground, dead. The street was empty, so there were no witnesses, but the unhurt youth claimed his friend hadn't done anything. The policeman alleged that the youth had made a movement like he was going for something inside his jacket. The dead kid had a clean record, and Callahan was handling this the same way he'd handled the project killings: He was conducting an

investigation while the policeman remained on desk duty. Even
though this was normal procedure, the black community was in an
uproar again, picketing outside Callahan's office, and wanted the
cop suspended from the force. Callahan refused to be interviewed.
He was in the right, but that didn't mean you had to like it if your
skin was black.

"You'd think Callahan would do somethin' so it at least *looks*
like he's got some sympathy," the old man said. "He's bein' just as
hard-nosed as ever."

"Something's going on," I said for the sake of conversation.

"Well, sure, there's *al*ways somethin'," he said impatiently. "But
that project mess is still hanging over him. Look, Neal, I'm a
cop"—he always says this like I never was and like he isn't
retired—"and I believe they had somethin' when they went into
the project that night, but what they did left a lot more questions
unanswered than answered, so it looks fishy. Right?" He didn't
wait for me to agree. "Now wit' this hap'nin'," he gestured toward
the newspaper, "Callahan's gonna come under fire again, and not
just for this, but for what happened at that project, too. It's not
that I underestimate Callahan, but if he has a black opponent who
can get the blacks out to vote, and he splits any of the white vote,
he could be in trouble."

That's because fifty-one percent of the registered voters in
Orleans Parish are black. I'd heard it all before—every time there
was an election.

"You know who's thinking of running against him?" I asked.
"Richard Cotton, the Colonel's son, Cotton National Bank."

"Oh, yeah? He's pretty young, isn't he?"

"He's smart, and he was a damned good prosecutor."

"Yeah, but it'll take someone older 'n stronger, wit' more
political experience to win against Callahan, I think. Unless he's
black."

We talked about it some more, and about what had happened at
Richard Cotton's house. I didn't need to tell the old man much
about that because Uncle Roddy had already filled him in.
"Rod'rick," as the old man calls him, acts like my father is still

with the department and consults him regularly. I was interested in how the cops were treating the Cotton business, and what the current theories were. The old man doesn't particularly like to confide in me about what the cops are doing since I'm not one anymore, but after a little circular talk, I gathered there was some thinking that it could have been an interrupted burglary, and that Cotton thought it was possible his key had been duplicated.

Well, I knew where *that* theory came from, so I knew Richard had been downtown talking to Uncle Roddy. Since the old man wasn't going to confide in me, I didn't think it would do any good to bring up the question of what burglar Uncle Roddy had ever heard of who'd interrupted himself to jump someone who was out in the front yard of the house he was burglarizing. But I also knew that neither my father nor Uncle Roddy were stupid cops who weren't thinking about that, or about the fire, either.

The old man sat back and lit a cigarette. "I noticed we ain't seen mucha you around here lately. Whereya been?" He asked in that way he has when he wants to know what's up with my love life. Well, more specifically, my sex life. He's given up on me ever doing anything normal like falling in love with someone I could marry. That's because of Myra. Therefore, it's my sex life he's referring to. I know how he thinks.

"I been hangin' around Audubon Park," I said, lighting up, too.

"What? It's freezin'!" He cocked one eyebrow. "You're not turnin' into one of them perverts, are you?"

I played the straight guy and told him I was seeing a woman who lived by the park. Then I mentioned that she was an investigator.

"What?" he demanded again. "The one at Cotton's house? Yeah, Rod'rick told me about her. Says she ain't built the way we used to like 'em"—he meant like Jane Russell or Betty Grable— "but she's got a way about her."

That last he said with his eyes squinted and his mouth pulled over to one side, which was probably supposed to look like Clark Gable and meant she was sexy even if she wasn't built like a 1940's movie queen.

"But, Jesus, Neal, doncha know better than to get in bed wit' a

woman cop, of any kind? Listen." He was ready for some
confidential talk now. He sat forward, and shuffled his feet around
to get them square on the floor, his moosehide slippers sounding
like brooms on the linoleum. "They're bad enough when you gotta
work wit' 'em."

"Aw, come on, Dad. Half the cops I knew who got married
when I was on the force married women cops."

"Ya heard about shotgun weddings, huh? Well, that's called a
.357 Magnum wedding."

"Who gives the bride away—Dirty Harry?"

He cracked a smile. "Lemme tell ya 'bout women cops." He
fueled up on a drag from his cigarette. "They're tough, you know,
but verrry sensitive." He put his hand over his heart. "Know
everything there is to know about human nature. And you? You
ain't sensitive at all. But lemme tell ya what. I seen many a man
throw up at the sight of a corpse, but very few women—in all
those years. They're *real* sensitive, about as sensitive as a block of
ice. And just as cold."

Yeah, well, Lee hadn't talked about it much, but she'd been
pretty upset over Raven's death. I think she thought she shouldn't
have been so disoriented even though she'd been hit in the head.

"Maybe they like to keep their feelings to themselves," I
suggested. "They don't like being called hysterical."

"Haw! Well, they don' mind gettin' hysterical if you say
anything about 'em bein' a woman!" He was getting excited. He
stood up. I could tell he was going into one of his acts. "They can
do whatever it is a man can do just as good as he can, and," he put
one hand on his hip and pointed at me with his cigarette, "don't
you forget it."

He pushed his chair back. "After they been in the profession
awhile, they get this kind of swagger." He stuck his cigarette in his
mouth, and did this tough-guy swagger around the kitchen. I tried
to imagine Lee Diamond swaggering.

"They're just one of the boys, right? But don't tell no dirty jokes
in front of 'em. That offends their precious, sensitive souls. All of
a sudden, they ain't swaggerin' no more. They're walkin' like

this." He prissed all around the table. In his thermal undershirt, pajama bottoms and moosehide slippers, it was just too much. I started laughing.

"Wait a minute! Wait a minute!" he yelled. He put his cigarette out in the dishwater. "You can't give 'em no advice. You do somethin' one way, they gotta better way. Somethin' don't go down right, you either, one"—he held up a finger—"weren't tough enough or, two"—another finger—"not compassionate enough. They always gotta be one up on you. It's like you been entered in some goddamn competition."

He was really getting wound up now. "So you finally decide that the best thing to do is to leave 'em alone. Then what happens?" He leaned on the table so he was closer to my face, which I was trying to keep straight, but not having much luck with. "They start makin' these funny eyes at you." He batted his eyelids up and down. "All of a sudden everything you say is just *so* funny. You're the most sensitive man they *ever* knew. They're askin' your advice when your advice wasn't worth two cents before. Before, you were a slob. There was gravy on your shirt. You needed a shave or a haircut. Now you're sexy as hell. The next thing you know, they got you in bed, but it's just for fun, no big deal. If it interferes wit' work, that's it. Everybody's happy for a while. Then you begin to notice they're psychic. They sense this, they sense that. You say one thing, they know you meant somethin' else."

I thought about Lee sensing that what Richard Cotton had said to me hadn't gone down quite right, but the comparison with what the old man was saying was so ridiculous that I couldn't hold the laughter in one more second. He liked my reaction. It egged him on.

"That's right! They not only know exactly what you think, they know exactly how you feel. They know it all!" he shrieked.

Yeah, I thought, just like you. But he didn't know Lee. He hadn't stood at Lee's front door with her that first night, and seen the way her eyes burned when she wanted me to kiss her. He also didn't know how mutual and immediate our attraction had been, how much we both wanted each other. He hadn't seen the look on her face after we made love. He hadn't run his hands down her long, smooth back. He hadn't heard her soft noises. I laughed even more at his foolishness.

He ran on. "Before you know it, though, you're not thinkin' what you oughta be thinkin' and you're not feelin' what you oughta be feelin'. There's somethin' wrong wit' your *attitude*. What's wrong wit' it is you ain't hot-footin' it off to the altar. You tell 'em they're rushin' it, and everything you ever said gets thrown in your face. Nex' thing, you're fightin' like cats and dogs, and it's all your fault. It's like *you* were the only one ready to hop in bed. Then when you try to call the whole thing off, what do they do? They start cryin', for God's sake!" He pitched his voice way up high and started boo-hooing. "'But, Neal, you said this was different. But, Neal, this, but Neal, that.'" He threw himself up against the refrigerator and sobbed into the crook of his arm.

At this point I was just about on the floor. I was begging him to stop.

It was quite a performance.

The old man. You know, he really is something.

8

The Murder
of Marty Solarno

I lived in a dream world during the next few weeks. Everything was easy. Witnesses were where they were supposed to be when I looked for them, and they were cooperative. A case I'd been working on with a lawyer finally went to court, and I handled the other side like Erle Stanley Gardner had written the lines for me. Another lawyer asked me to subpoena someone no one else had been able to find. I found him in two hours. No one asked me to do anything too sleazy. I was getting along with the old man as well as I ever had in my life.

Most evenings I left the office and went over to Dumaine Street to pick up Lee. We found so many new places to go that I started thinking of New Orleans as an exciting place to be instead of a place where nothing changes. I wasn't drinking so much anymore, and I wasn't missing it either. Lee had me working out with weights. What I liked best about it was watching her do it, but it gave me a lot of extra stamina for when stamina counts the most, and I liked that, too. We were always at her place at the beginning, but when the heat got fixed and stayed fixed at the Euclid, we started spending some of our time there. I wanted equal time on my territory even if the territory was shabby. But Lee said it was convenient to be so much closer to downtown and our offices. So even the Euclid was okay.

The trouble with dream worlds is that you wake up.

· · ·

It started one morning that was just like any other morning. I parked in the garage at the Père Marquette, and exchanged a few words with Gabe, the garage attendant. As usual, we complained about the weather, and Gabe gave me the forecast past a toothpick that miraculously stays put on his lower lip no matter how wide he opens his mouth. Then I went into the sandwich shop on the ground floor of the building to get a cup of coffee from Leone, who can be very abusive during the early morning rush hour. She demanded to know what right I had to be so happy lately. When I grinned and winked at her, she accused me of being secretive, then snarled that she'd get it out of me, which she would if I ever went in there when she wasn't flying around behind the counter. I grabbed the coffee, got a copy of the *Picayune*, and went up to the office.

I read the opening paragraphs on the top half of the front page, and when I flipped the paper over, there was Marty Solarno's mug smiling at me. I realized right then that one of the reasons I was so happy lately was that I was managing to get through whole days without seeing Myra Ledet's slashed throat, her blood all over the bed I'd spent a lot of time in with her, her mouth wide open in death, the terrified scream I knew must have come from her stopped by somebody's knife. Possibly Solarno's.

Solarno was dead. He'd been murdered, most grotesquely: His body was full of stab wounds and his face had been carved like a Halloween pumpkin's. As far as I was concerned, it was a fitting death if he'd had anything to do with Myra's murder.

One reason Solarno's picture made the front page of the paper was because he was notorious around town, the way a bad bed of oysters is notorious. For years Solarno could be found at the center of any smut that was going on in New Orleans. If it took too long to get from one kind of smut to the next, Solarno invented his own. Or maybe he didn't. Sometimes it was hard to tell. If there was a hot trial about to happen, you could start placing your bets that Solarno would be a witness for the prosecution, if not the star witness. Marty Solarno was a media hound, and he didn't like it if too much time passed without his getting enough attention from the press. None of this, of course, guarantees that you'll get a front-page story just because you're murdered, not unless you happened to be both Angelesi's and Callahan's chief investigator.

I knew Myra had been sleeping with Angelesi, and I didn't like it. Myra's profession and the fact that she wouldn't give it up came close to unhinging me several times because I was in love with her and wanted to marry her. But I didn't have enough money for Myra, and even though I moved back home to save for the big, fine house I was going to buy her, the truth of it was I probably never would have had enough money for Myra's tastes. Okay, so Myra was mercenary, but she was also beautiful and smart, and no one had a better time than the two of us together. No one could laugh like Myra could laugh; no one could make me laugh like she did. But Myra got a little too mercenary for her own good.

She told me that at the beginning Angelesi couldn't get off unless he talked about power first, what a powerful district attorney he was. She thought it was funny. Gradually, he began to tell her exactly how powerful he was and what it meant to him in terms of cash. He was taking payoffs from the pinball people, from bookmakers, some large call-girl operations, a few drug dealers. He had even stooped to blackmailing a couple of judges who wanted their sexual preferences to remain closeted away from the public.

But it was Marty Solarno who had the nose. Wherever there was a vice operation, he sniffed it out, collected the bribes, and got part of the take for his trouble. He even conducted a raid every once in a while. Maybe one of the reasons Solarno liked to keep a high profile was to keep from getting bumped off, because the amazing thing was that he hadn't been taken out by someone before now. He did the dirty work so that Angelesi could keep his hands clean. Anyway, Myra decided that there was enough money being passed around that she deserved a few extra bucks for lending an ear.

When she told me what she was doing, I flipped. We had a terrible argument and said some pretty nasty things to each other. At one point I told her that what she was doing could only mean that she had absolutely no self-esteem. For some reason that really got to her. She stopped screaming at me; she stopped saying anything at all to me; she wouldn't look at me. There was some kind of deep, miserable pain all over her face, and all I could think was I had caused it. I went over to her, got down beside the chair she was sitting in, and took her hands.

"Myra," I said, "however much money it is that Angelesi is giving you, let me give it to you instead."

It took awhile, then she put her eyes on me, her mouth curved up on one side, and she let go with one of those laughs. "You go home and save your money," she hissed.

I stood up and slugged her. I never in my life felt so bad about anything—never, that is, until I unlocked her door that night and found her with her throat cut.

I stared at the picture of Solarno, and all the rage and hate I'd felt five years ago rushed back with a vengeance. I was feeling nearly sick from it. I probably should have felt some gratitude, too, though, for still being alive. I went after Angelesi. I wanted to tear his throat out. And every time I tried, it was Solarno who stopped me. I remembered his big, thick hands on me, pounding on me, with revulsion. He was two of me. He could have killed me if he'd wanted to.

Solarno saved his own hide by becoming the "surprise" witness for the prosecution at Angelesi's trial. He must have done some slick maneuvering. Then he stayed on as chief investigator for Callahan, but not for long. All it took was Solarno giving out one of his own brand of "press release," this time that cops were getting bribe money in their paychecks, as usual unsubstantiated, and Callahan got rid of him. Callahan was either too smart or too corrupt to keep Solarno around. It was hard to tell which.

I threw the newspaper in the trash can to get that easy smile of

Solarno's out of my sight. I sat back in the chair and closed my eyes. The floodgates had been released on all of my worst feelings, most brutal the anguish of my own helplessness to stop them or ever be rid of them. There was the added horror of what the repetition of those feelings had done to my most base and savage impulses, so that the only way to make things better was to rip flesh and crush bones. I had to talk myself out of this, as I'd done a thousand times before. After all, it had been my own loudness and persistence that was responsible for bringing Angelesi to trial, but he'd been tried and convicted for bribe taking and racketeering, not for Myra's murder.

Now Solarno was dead, but he had died without anyone knowing how much of Myra's blood was on his hands. I suddenly realized that I had something more powerful than images of Angelesi rotting in jail or Solarno's carved face to get some relief from this.

I had Lee. I concentrated on her, I saw her face, alive with laughter, intense with passion, soft with satisfaction. I saw her flesh moving over her straining muscles as she worked out, moving and shimmering underneath me. I heard her voice, wistful with memories, strong and logical as we discussed some real or hypothetical case, soft as it caught in her throat when we made love. I could feel her hands all over me. I wanted her right now. I wanted to go over to her office and take her without a word or an explanation, just take her, hard and fast and brutally, then long and slow and steadily, until there was nothing left in my brain but her. These were impulses I didn't have to control. If I wanted her now, I could have her. There was no schedule of other men. Nothing stood in our way, least of all Lee's profession.

Thinking like that made me feel better. I thought I could do a day's work now. I thought, in fact, with some satisfaction, that I was on the way to conquering the past even if I couldn't forget it.

And then the phone rang. It was Richard Cotton.

"Did you see the morning paper?" he asked. I put the

mouthpiece under my chin, blew out a lungful of air, and told him that I had.

"You've got to do something for me," he said urgently. "You've got to find out what Solarno had on Callahan."

9

Fish
Out of Water

"Y ou've got to be shitting me."

I don't usually say things like that to people I work for, but Richard had just told me that he'd hired Marty Solarno to dig up every piece of dirt he could find on Chance Callahan.

"Excuse me, Richard," I went on, "but don't you know that Solarno was untrustworthy at best, and probably nuts? He could have told you anything, but that wouldn't mean it was true."

"No. I told Solarno that anything he gave me, there had to be evidence. He called yesterday and said he had something I could use and the stuff to prove it."

"What kind of stuff?"

Richard didn't know. Solarno had called him and said he had something to show him. They had set up a meeting at Solarno's place for this afternoon.

"Damn!" Richard cried suddenly. "I should have met him last night. Paula had us going to another damned Mardi Gras ball."

"You're not thinking straight, buddy. You better go home and tell Paula how grateful you are she made those plans."

"Paula doesn't know anything about any of this," he said quickly.

"Just the point I was trying to make," I said. "Why are you going after Callahan like this, Richard?"

He gave a sarcastic laugh. "You don't honestly think I can win against him on my youth and experience, do you?"

"No, but why can't you use what everybody already knows about, the project killings and how Callahan's got the investigation corked on that kid who got gunned down. The blacks are angry. Why can't you go after their votes?"

"I will, but Callahan will make that look like Jay Gatsby going after their votes."

"What about the whites uptown who think they aren't getting enough police protection?"

"I can't win with just the uptown vote. Be realistic, Neal. No politician wins on smiles and handshakes anymore. And don't forget it was you who brought up the man in my fireplace. That hasn't been cleared up and it's not likely to get cleared up before the campaign starts, or ever, for that matter. Without a new lead, the police won't spend any more time on it."

"Okay. But why Solarno?"

"Who better than Solarno?"

"I hope you realize that if you persist with this you could end up like Solarno. So could I."

"You went after Angelesi, and you're still around."

"Wait a minute. What I meant is Solarno was everything from a pimp to a bagman. He knew a nasty bunch of people. What are you trying to say—that Callahan killed him?"

There was a silence during which I assumed he was trying to decide how far he should commit himself. Instead he asked me a question. "If I were to say to you that by the time Callahan fired Solarno, Solarno's name was a joke around town, so why would Callahan bother killing him, what kind of idiot would you call me?"

I almost laughed, but it wouldn't have come out sounding like a laugh. After all, why would Angelesi bother to kill the likes of Myra? Hadn't everyone asked me that, including my own father?

"So now what—you want me to go after Callahan?"

His voice got a little thin, his words a little drawn out. "I hired Solarno to do a job. From what he told me yesterday, he did it. I'd like to know what he had. I'm asking you to find out. To ask you to do anything else would be stupid."

I supposed he was getting impatient with me, but I didn't care. "What am I looking for, Richard? You told me a while back you thought Callahan was getting rich off some vice operations. Is that it?"

"Drugs and vice. I've suspected for a long time that Callahan has a large interest in a local drug operation. He's gotten too rich for it to be anything other than drugs. I've been trying to find out anything I can, where the drugs are dropped, who is involved. Then I could go to the police. But as it is I have nothing to go to them with except some vague suspicions."

"How do you know Callahan has anything to do with it? Where did you get your information, from Solarno?"

"How I know has nothing to do with what we're doing now."

"I doubt that. I doubt that very seriously, Richard. Look, when I went after Angelesi, I had nothing to lose. I could tell anybody who would listen what I thought. We're not in that position now. And we've always been up-front with each other before. This is a hell of a time to start playing it cozy."

"I'm not trying to play it cozy, and I am trying to be up-front. What I know did not come from Solarno. It came from personal experience, when I was on Angelesi's staff."

"I think you better tell me about it."

Richard was good at letting you hang on the phone. But then I'm good at waiting.

Finally, he said, "Do you remember a time in your life when you thought it was okay to be a little reckless, when you got involved in something because you thought getting involved was the only way to play the game? What you're too stupid to know is that everything you do becomes a part of you, and that the things you do have insidious ways of coming back on you. If you know what I mean, then don't ask me to embarrass myself by getting any more specific."

I knew what he meant. Didn't I say it before? *Simpático*. But there was another dimension to what he was talking about:

Sometimes you got involved because you had no choice. I didn't choose to meet Myra, fall in love with her, and find her murdered. The problem was that the longer I talked to Richard, the more I got the feeling that one of those things was coming back on me, too.

He was saying, "I guarantee you that the way I found out what I know about Callahan in no way affects what I'm asking you to do." I believed him because that was such a nice, qualified statement, a limited guarantee. "I'm just asking you to do what you can. Find out what the police know. Use your contacts. Get into Solarno's apartment. I'm asking you to do this as a personal favor to me."

"There's one thing you better understand," I told him. "If I get into Solarno's apartment, it's not likely I'll find anything that the police have missed, but if I should find anything that's evidence of a crime, I'm going to the police with it."

"Fair enough," he said.

"Then there's one more thing. It has to do with things coming back on you. My advice is leave it alone. Let whatever it is die with Solarno."

Richard paused, then said quietly, "What if there's evidence of another crime—should it die, too? It's not too late, you know."

He was baiting me. I fully realized how ambivalent I felt about all of this. On the one hand, I was already getting a bad taste scrambling around in the past. On the other, if there was something else to know about Myra's death, I couldn't say I didn't want to know it. I also knew there wasn't any way of digging around in Solarno's life without hoping that there was. It was coming back on me, all right.

Solarno had been murdered in his Bourbon Street apartment. The French Quarter was part of Uncle Roddy's district, and with a phone call I could find out if Solarno's murder was Uncle Roddy's case. It probably was. I already knew what I could say to get Uncle Roddy to let me into Solarno's apartment, but I did not like the idea of saying it at all.

A small shudder went through me. I'm superstitious sometimes, and this was one of those times. So I told Richard that I was doing this as a personal favor to him. In fact, I did regard it as a favor to a friend, not as taking on a case. And then I told him about how at any moment I might call him and say I wasn't doing it anymore.

But here it is in a nutshell: He supplied the bait and I took it.

10

Memories and Delusions

After I got off the phone with Richard Cotton, I finished my paperwork to avoid thinking about what exactly it was I was going to do about this Solarno business. I updated several files and wrote out a few statements. Then I put some letters and other things that needed to be typed into the Dictaphone machine so I could take the tape and the statements around the corner to a typing service I used. It was cheaper than a secretary.

Once I had all that done, I had nothing to do but get used to thinking about Marty Solarno again. I would take it one step at a time. First, the rational part of myself told the irrational part that if the old obsession about Myra's death so much as threatened to take over, I would immediately call Richard Cotton and bow out. Second, I would indulge in no idle speculation over who had murdered Solarno; I would go after what I had been asked to go after, and nothing else. Third, I put a call in to Uncle Roddy, but discovered he was out of the office on the Solarno case.

It would probably be bad timing to try to see Uncle Roddy during the height of an investigation, anyway. Not only that, but before I approached Uncle Roddy, it would be helpful to know some specifics about the kind of life Solarno had been leading. I knew exactly who I could go see, but I didn't like at all where I had to go to find him.

I had to go to Dumaine Street, and I was feeling superstitious again—Tom Rivers' lounge, The Ace, was a block away from Lee's office.

I wasn't sure I wanted Lee to know anything about Myra. Very few people had understood my obsession with Myra and her murder. I was afraid to tell Lee about it. It had caused me nothing but trouble and, anyway, why should the woman I was currently involved with be very understanding about a woman I was once in love with who was a prostitute? I could think that, and at the same time I knew if I ever did tell Lee and she didn't understand, it would make me angry. I felt so strongly that I didn't want what had happened with Myra to touch my relationship with Lee. I felt so strongly that I didn't even like the idea of The Ace being on the same street as Lee's office.

Myra and I had spent a lot of time in The Ace. It was our favorite bar. It was near enough to her place on Esplanade that we could walk to it, and Tom Rivers would stay open all night if he had a customer. There was a lot of action, too. One of the local TV stations was right around the corner, and after the late news most of the reporters and crew would go to The Ace. Myra used to feel sorry for the weatherman because everyone who walked into The Ace asked him how the weather was, and as the night wore on he would hang lower and lower over his drink.

With the media making the scene at The Ace, Tom Rivers had another regular—Marty Solarno. One night he brought Angelesi with him. I told Myra if she so much as looked at him, I was leaving.

Anyway, there was always an interesting crowd. And even though the place was comfortable and nice, the real reason they all came to The Ace was Tom Rivers himself. He was a quiet man, observant. He was on the small side, and the only thing left on his head was a sparse fringe of blondish hair and a few freckles. In spite of his middle age and baldness, there was something boyish about Tom Rivers. He had never developed that hardness that some bar owners get after years of running a drinking establish-ment, but retained a vulnerability and sensitivity that I, at any rate, associate with youth. He remembered everyone's name and listened well, as any good bartender should, and was a man of few words. He never, as far as I could remember, talked about himself, his family or friends, nor could I remember ever seeing him alone with anyone. Maybe it was this quality of mystery that made Tom Rivers so attractive and so easy to confide in. It was as if he and The Ace were one and the same, and whatever you told him would never go beyond the four-sided bar that dominated the room. The nightly ritual was that whenever Rivers finished his work, he would make his way around the bar once, carrying his drink with him and studying it while he listened to one outpouring or another. Then he would disappear and let his bartenders close up.

As I walked over to Dumaine Street, I was hoping, for once, that things hadn't changed, that the rituals at The Ace were still being observed, that Tom Rivers still arrived around three o'clock to get ready for his five o'clock crowd, and that Marty Solarno, up until he died, had still been bending Tom Rivers' ear. But it had been well over three years since I'd been to The Ace or seen Tom Rivers, and the way bars come and go in this otherwise museum of a city, it was possible he wasn't there anymore.

I pushed open the door, and as much as I'd been hoping he'd be right where he was, bent down behind the bar checking his supplies, I felt that ambivalence creeping over me, intruding on my genuine pleasure of seeing the familiar face of someone I considered a friend. It wasn't seeing Tom Rivers, though, it was the place itself. Nothing at all seemed to have changed. The memories were all there, ghostlike visions that at once beckoned me in and pushed me away.

The bar was nearly empty—only two people sitting at a far corner. Rivers stood up to see who was coming in, and when he saw it was me, he smiled, maybe a little wider than usual, but a small smile, never a grin.

"Neal, how you doin'?" It was his same quiet greeting, never boisterous, as if I'd just been in yesterday, except it was a little slowed down, drawn out by surprise, maybe. Or it could have been that Rivers was a few years older and that much slower. He put his palms on the bar and leaned on them. We didn't shake hands because Rivers never shook hands with anybody. "Been a long time," he said.

I sat on a stool in front of him.

"Too long. I'm glad to see you, Rivers. I thought you might be gone."

He let his eyes wander around the room. "No. I'm still here, but if you'd waited too much longer to come in, I might not have been. You know that beach house everyone always liked to talk about? Well, it exists now. I'm thinking about selling out and retiring."

"What?" I demanded in mock disbelief. "There was no beach house, no poker game?"

The beach house and the poker game were another Ace ritual. The story went that Rivers had won The Ace in an all-night poker game. Only three people were left in the game and one of the other two men had won all the cash from Rivers and the previous owner of the lounge. The winner offered to play one more hand if Rivers and the bar owner could come up with something worth betting on. The bar owner put up his bar, and Rivers put up all he had in the world, his house on the Gulf Coast, and, so the story went, his peace of mind. The game was five card draw and Rivers was dealt everything he needed for a royal flush except the ace. He asked for one card and got both the card and the place.

No one knew exactly how the story had originated, except it was the kind of story Tom Rivers himself might have told after one drink too many. But whenever someone could add something new and clever to the story about The Ace, Tom Rivers would order Schnapps for everyone at the bar and make a toast, "To our unmade memories, and all of our delusions." Everyone would down the Schnapps in one gulp and be extremely pleased with the performance of the ritual. Maybe it was Tom Rivers' routines and rituals that gave The Ace its staying power—there were no surprises here. Myra, the romantic she could be sometimes, loved the ritual of the Schnapps and Rivers' toast. She thought it was poetic and was fond of quoting it, especially whenever I talked about our future together.

"And not too much more Schnapps going around either," Rivers said, "but enough for us." He reached behind him, got a bottle off the shelf, and poured Schnapps up to the little white lines on two shot glasses. He raised his glass and started to speak.

"Don't say it," I said.

We both tossed the liquor down our throats. My eyes were still watering when he asked, "So what brings you around, Neal? Is it Marty Solarno?"

Tom Rivers never did miss much.

"Was he still coming around, Rivers?"

"Not as much as he used to, but some."

"Do you know who he was hanging with, what he was doing?"

Rivers stared at me and I could see little gears clicking behind his eyeballs. It wasn't his style to question me, or anyone. And I figured it was a fifty-fifty chance that he would tell me he knew nothing. He was measuring his reply like he measured the Schnapps. He blinked and said, "Do you know Mr. D.'s Laundry over on Bourbon?" I told him I'd never noticed it. "It's a hole in the wall in the same block as Solarno's apartment. You have to call and make an appointment with Mr. D. Danny Dideaux's his name." He blinked again. "Try not to tell him I sent you."

11

Monuments
to the Past

Mr. D.'s Laundry, at just after four o'clock in the afternoon, was closed, a small padlock on the front door. Through a smudgy storefront window, I peered into the dim interior. One giant step from the window was a counter. Beyond it was a rod that stretched from one wall to the other, maybe eight feet across, that was about a third full of hanging clothes. Most of the clothes were pushed to the right side, but only a few of them were covered in those thin plastic garment bags. Behind the rod was a greenish wall mottled by peeling paint, cracked plaster and dinge. The whole place was just a big closet, ill-kept, and probably closed most of the time. But I guessed it was all Mr. D. needed to show he had a legitimate income.

I moved several inches so that I was standing at the far left of the window, my eyes still on the clothes all huddled together, discarded props shoved out of the way. But that's not at all what they were. They were camouflage. Without most of my body blocking what little daylight could get through the dirty window, I saw the two straight lines that met at a right angle just above the rod, a narrow door covered by shirts and dresses that could have come from a rummage sale. And what went on behind the green door? Take your pick—gambling, bookmaking, pimping, drug pushing, peep shows, blackmail setups, maybe a little bit of everything. Whatever you chose you could bet it was a good deal more profitable for Mr. D. than his laundry.

I turned around and looked across the street at the police unit pulled up on the sidewalk in front of a door that must have gone to Marty Solarno's apartment. The door was sandwiched between two strip joints. One of the buildings had a big window on its front, rigged so that at night a girl could get up on a velvet-covered swing and jut her stockinged legs back and forth through the opening. Lined up on the window's ledge were beer cans, plastic cups, hot dog wrappers, even a corn cob from the Corn King down the street. Why remove the sleaze when it would just be put back there the next night?

The whole block, Solarno's neighborhood, was a depressing sight. It stayed trashed-out most of the time because not many people cared if they littered in front of enterprises that made money by appealing to the lust, lewdness and weakness for bathroom humor that occupies a space, no matter how small, in most of us. The most chaste and upright sightseer could come to Bourbon Street and have a raunchy, unembarrassed guffaw, and go home still chaste and upright. Or if you didn't like it, you could go home and shake your head and tell about the sinful, appalling things that go on in the world. If you really didn't like it, you could stand out on a corner and preach against it. It stays here and it thrives because it's in all of us in one form or another.

But that's just what's out front, what you can see. It's the stuff that goes on behind closed doors, like Mr. D.'s green door, that gets scary. That's where the action can become addictive, where there's no love, only fornication and sexual abuse, no satisfaction in work, just greed. Where people get their faces carved and their throats cut.

Yeah, and which corner are you going to rent, I asked myself.

I started walking back to Dumaine Street, wishing I'd never met Myra, that what happened to her had not become a part of me.

I should have called Lee and told her I was sick with the malaise, or gangrene of the mind, anything, but instead I went on to her office, faithful as always. I hadn't learned yet that good qualities, like faithfulness and persistence, can be taken too far, to no one's benefit. I was, to say the least, a bit on the morose side. She wasn't waiting in the doorway; she was closed up in her office. I sat behind the desk in the waiting room. One of the buttons on the phone was lit. I'd had a few vague thoughts about Lee's high-rent setup before, but I looked around me with a much colder eye now. It was all done very simply, but that didn't mean it was inexpensive. She hardly ever used the upstairs accommodations, though maybe she'd spent more time there before I came along. She kept up two luxury apartments, two cars, and she had a closetful of expensive clothes that she treated rather carelessly. I let the thought go uninterrupted across my brain that it just went to show what some higher education and deceased parents could do for you, which I admit just to give you an idea about my state of mind.

Another fifteen minutes passed. I lit my seventh cigarette, and fired up my irritation. When Lee came out of her office, I didn't get up. She walked over and kissed me.

"You won't have much wind left for a good workout," she remarked.

I shrugged. "I don't feel like working out. I want to go home and eat steaks."

I know Lee doesn't like to break her routine, but after only a moment she said, "Okay."

The first thing I did after I opened the door to the apartment was hit the kitchen and fix a double Scotch. I made short work of that one and immediately fixed another. Lee watched me pour it, then went into the bedroom and turned on the TV. I drank the second one slower while I threw potatoes in the oven, washed lettuce, and seasoned the steaks. I was feeling a bit lighter now.

When the news was over, Lee came into the kitchen. She started dressing the salad; her dressings are better than mine.

She said conversationally, "The police say they have no leads on Marty Solarno's murder." I held back the sigh that tried to escape. Then she said in a rather familiar way, "I wonder what he was up to *this* time. He was really crazy."

I had too much alcohol in me to jump exactly. "Did you know him?"

The quickness of my question turned her around. "No. Did you?"

"Yeah. He might have been more mean than crazy."

"Why? What did he do to you?"

"Well, let's see. One time he broke my nose." I put my finger over the rise on its bridge. "Another time he kicked the shit out of me, cracked a couple of ribs and bruised my pancreas. That was the worst."

Her eyebrows scaled their way up her forehead. "Why? What did you do to him?"

"Oh, I might have given him a pain in his big beefy jaw for about two hours."

"No. I mean, why did he do that to you?"

"I don't want to talk about it."

She didn't push it. She took over in the kitchen while I had another drink, smaller this time. But as she took the skillet out, she closed the cabinet door a little harder than necessary. And when she got the potatoes out of the oven, she almost threw the rack back in it. Her face, however, was impassive. I couldn't help it; I started enjoying myself. I enjoyed seeing the definition of her thigh against her tight wool skirt when she bent down, her slender fingers slinging the hair out of her face, her quick, strong arm as she lifted the steaks and tossed them over in the pan with the expertise of a chef at Charlie's Steak House. I might have even started smiling a little, but she didn't so much as glance at me.

We made about two comments to each other while we ate and cleaned up. I went into the living room and sat on the sofa. She went to the window and looked down on St. Charles Avenue.

"Lee. Come over here."

She took her time, but sat down next to me. "What's bothering you, Neal?"

I put my fingers in her hair and let them run down through it to her shoulder where they stopped for a caress before moving to her bicep, making a circle, not quite all the way, around it. I kissed her and her arm went up around my neck and she kissed me back, as responsive as ever. But when we broke apart, the question was still on her face.

I pushed the sleeve of her close-fitting cashmere sweater up and stroked her forearm. "This town can be a damned peculiar place," I said. "It's so provincial that sometimes it seems like not more than about a thousand people live here. It's hard to go anywhere without seeing someone you know. People live out their entire lives in one neighborhood. I met an old woman once who lived on Burgundy Street in the French Quarter, in the same house she'd been born in. She'd never gone across Canal Street, and saw no reason to. Then you've got the people uptown who think Metairie is a dirty word because everything there is new. They've got all these codes and standards that they live by and judge other people by, that they've carried with them for generations. No amount of money or success can make you one of them.

"Take Maurice, for example. He's one of the best-known lawyers in town and he's lived in the Garden District most of his life. But his ancestors aren't from here, and the house he lives in was built in the 1950's, not the 1850's. He's nouveau riche. That's a dirty word, too." I was pretty wound up. "That kind of thinking isn't confined to just the uppercrust, though. They think the same way in the Channel. All the young professionals who are moving in and renovating houses are sneered at. They're outsiders. And even the renovators are snobs. They're all trying to beat each other to the oldest houses. The whole city is like a monument to the past, and the way people live is a tribute to it."

"And that's what's bothering you?" Lee asked incredulously. "That people try to preserve their past and their heritage? There's another side to what you're talking about, you know."

"I know," I said, "but you've just been treated to one of my favorite diatribes." She smiled and that upper lip did something to my insides. But I wanted her to understand.

"Look, I don't think people should throw away their past. But I don't think it should rule them either. Look at my old man—he's a great one for family tradition. He's never going to get over the fact that I'm not a cop anymore. He thinks I should be because he was a cop and my grandfather was a cop. I broke the tradition, and he doesn't like it, and he lets me know it. I'm an outcast, a deviant. I'm not a good son."

"You're talking about families now, Neal, not a town," Lee said reasonably.

"But the town has something to do with it. When you're surrounded by the past, when everything is so old, tradition runs deep and your roots grow deep, especially if where you're from means anything at all to you. Maybe it's hard for you to understand because you didn't grow up here. Your roots aren't here. Richard Cotton would know exactly what I'm talking about, and we're from different sides of the track. He probably wishes he never had to go to another Mardi Gras ball, but he'll keep going to them because it's expected of him, because Mardi Gras is as much a part of his family tradition and heritage as it is the town's." I was just about played out.

"Hm," was all Lee said.

I was beginning to get a headache from all this deep thinking, and it didn't look as if she understood, anyway. "Richard called me today," I told her, "and asked me to do something for him."

"Ah, so you're a detective with a case again."

"Not exactly. I'm doing him a favor. I deliberately put it on a very informal basis because what he asked me to do is going to have me scrounging around in my past, and I'm not sure I'm going to like it. If I don't, then he can get somebody else, and there'll be no hard feelings."

Lee cupped her chin in her palm, and her fingers beat a light tattoo on her cheek. "So it was Richard Cotton's phone call that's got you brooding about the past and slugging down alcohol and chain-smoking cigarettes?"

I didn't like her tone of voice at all. I took my hands off her. "Look, Lee, I've been trying my best to get you to understand. It was the best I could do."

"Why don't you try telling me exactly what it is about the past? Why can't you talk in concrete terms instead of all these abstractions about codes and traditions?"

"Because I think it would be bad luck."

"You're superstitious, too?"

I got up and went around the cocktail table. "Yeah," I said. "I brood and I'm superstitious." I didn't say it very pleasantly either. Now she stood up. She folded her arms. "Neal, are you afraid to tell me something about your past? Are you afraid it's going to cause trouble between us?" She said it very calmly; I didn't like being talked to like I was an adolescent.

"It looks like it already has."

"No, it hasn't. We see things differently, that's all. I see this city as being old and charming, not rancid with the past."

That word "rancid" grated on me. "That's because you didn't grow up here." I wasn't going to give her a break. Stubbornness instead of blood runs in the Raffertys' veins. And, okay, the booze in my system was probably making me belligerent.

"I can't help that," she said sharply, but her face was a mask of self-control. "I think all this talk about the past is self-indulgent."

"Oh. Self-indulgent."

"Yes." She wasn't going to give me a break either. She came around the other side of the cocktail table, and said in that matter-of-fact way of hers, "I don't see the world like you do; I don't look for the ironies and the negative associations. I don't speculate about what the people on the other side of the tracks think, and I don't judge anybody because they like old houses better than new ones. I go for the facts and I don't miss them for being sentimental." She was not riled or ruffled in any way.

But I was. "Go ahead. Add sentimental to the list of what's wrong with me. Judgmental, too. I do tend to make judgments about the way people die, and I get sentimental, too." I was almost shouting.

A quizzical look passed over her face, then it was gone. "Marty Solarno?" she asked.

I shouted back, "No, I am not sentimental about Marty Solarno!"

Her face was completely unemotional, but there was that tenseness in her body, that same readiness I'd seen in her the first night at Richard Cotton's house. It moved her over to the windows again. She stood with her back to me, saying nothing more.

I went into the kitchen to get another drink, but as I started pouring it into the glass, I thought better of it. Exactly what I'd never wanted to happen was happening, and it was happening for exactly the reason I hadn't wanted it to. Hadn't I just finished telling Lee that people shouldn't let the past rule them?

I walked back into the living room and put my hands on her shoulders. "I'm sorry I yelled at you." I kissed her hair, moved it, and kissed her neck. She didn't react. I wanted to start the night over again. I wanted to be with her, just the two of us without this other monument to the past, that I had put there, between us. I turned her around.

"I'm going now," she said.

And then she was gone, so fast that I almost looked around the room, surprised I was alone.

Back in the kitchen I poured out a drink and thought about going over to Grady's, a bar in the Channel, to play a few games of pool, but I never did. Instead I sat around drinking, and thinking about how Lee and I saw the world differently, and how we got angry in such different ways. Any thoughts I might have had to make sense of it all got booze-soaked, and anything I was going to do about any of it I would have to face later.

But as I sat there I started feeling very contrite, and after a while I called her. She wasn't home, and her answering service got the phone at her office. I realized I had no idea where she would have gone or who she might be with. For all the time we'd spent together, we were still strangers.

I eventually went to bed, and fell into a drunken, fitful sleep only after I had the thought that the way you get to know someone better is by testing your relationship. And that made me think that the way you get to know yourself better is by testing your limitations.

12

A Diamond
Before You Die

I called Mr. D.'s Laundry intermittently most of the day with no luck. So I decided to try my luck instead with Uncle Roddy.

The district headquarters downtown was in more of a frenzy of activity than usual. Over the previous weekend, the Mardi Gras season had been kicked off officially with the rolling of several parades. All over town the mood was different, there was more traffic, more people on the streets, more drinking and carousing and visitors in a city famous for drinking and carousing and visitors. The gaiety and boisterousness would reach a pitch on the coming weekend, and stay there until Fat Tuesday itself, when the wall-to-wall crowds on Canal Street could be parted only by the oncoming tandem of floats, and the din would be deafening citywide.

The din was deafening in the police station and the mood was different there, too. Most of the cops do double shifts during Mardi Gras, and I could already see some signs of overwork and irritation, but I could also hear a lot of joking and laughing. It's the only way to cope when you know that what faces you after very little sleep is having to see trouble before it starts in the midst of several thousand partying people.

Even in the middle of the week before Mardi Gras, the station was already getting its share of costumed visitors. One of them was an old drunk decked out in silver stockings and grape leaves. He was sleeping it off on a bench in the glutted hallway, clutching a brown paper bag like the bottle was still inside it. At the side of a desk across the hall sat two young teenagers with painted faces. The officer who'd brought them in, probably for sleeping on the street, was trying to get the girl to tell him where she was from, but all she was doing was crying. The tears weren't disturbing the gold glitter all around her eyes, but the bright red star painted high on one cheekbone was beginning to run like streaks of blood. The boy's eyes glowed with defiance, bright spots in a sinister mask of black and purple face paint.

I made my way through the chaos, cracking wise with some of the guys I knew, to Uncle Roddy's office. Just as I got to his closed office door, Fonte emerged. He shoved a stick of gum folded in thirds into his mouth, and blocked the door.

"What trouble brings you in, Rafferty?" I could tell he'd been putting in his time with Uncle Roddy—he was beginning to sound like him.

"I'd like to see the lieutenant, Phil."

I don't think he liked my use of his first name. His upper lip curled. "Whadaya want?"

"To see the lieutenant."

His mouth worked the gum, then rolled it up into his cheek. "Whatsa matter? Aren't any of the uptown richies' wives foolin' around on 'em?"

"I know you don't like me or what I do very much, Fonte, but you know what? It's all right. It really is all right." Before he had time to compute an answer to that, I added, "Do you think it would be okay if I saw Lieutenant Rankin now, Sergeant?"

I thought I was going to have to indulge him in some more standoff time, but he shrugged and said, "It's up to him if he wants to see you," and walked off.

I knocked once and let myself in.

Uncle Roddy was on the phone. He looked up at me and pointed to the chair in front of his desk. I sat down.

"So that's it?" he said into the phone. His low-slung eyelids hit bottom and came up slowly. "Yeah, I'd love to know what the bastard had for dinner." He listened, grunted, and hung up. "Jesus, those pathologists are disgusting, and they don't even know it. What can I do for you, Neal?"

It's hard to know how to play Uncle Roddy. Sometimes a stall tactic works best, softens him up; other times your best shot is a direct hit. But all of a sudden I realized that I didn't give a damn what his reaction was or what he thought of me. I didn't feel like playing games, so I hit him. "I'd like to get into Marty Solarno's apartment."

There was no real reaction. He just wanted to know why.

My brain went into a kind of muddle: First I wished I'd opted for some stall time to psyche myself up; then I wanted to be alone so I could call Richard Cotton and tell him I was out; then I was remembering a drunken thought about testing my limitations. Then I was saying, "Myra Ledet."

Air whistled past his nostrils. "I shouldof known."

Uncle Roddy knew as well as anybody, better than most, how obsessed I'd been. He'd been the one who'd told me to resign from the NOPD before they tossed me.

He leaned toward me over the desk. I steeled myself for some verbal abuse. "Neal, you're gonna have to get over this one day," he said quietly.

I think my face managed not to register shock at how reasonable he sounded. "I know, Uncle Roddy. I'm trying."

"But what could you possibly expect to find in Marty Solarno's apartment now?" He turned his big hands over, his fingers splayed wide.

"I don't know."

"I mean, Neal, we been over that place wit' a fine-tooth comb." His shoulders grew larger as he hunched them up around his neck. "Tell me—would you expect to find anything in there if she'd just been killed yesterday?"

"No, probably not."

"You gotta move on. It won't do you no good to go in there." His eyes left my face and started wandering over the mass of papers on his desk. I was about to get the big kiss-off.

"You know, Uncle Roddy, you don't get over something like that by being forced to turn your back on it. Every time I've ever tried to get close enough to the situation so I could deal with it in my own way, there's been somebody there to stop me."

I said it mildly enough, but I had his attention again.

"Consider that you were being saved from yourself," he said.

"Yeah, like Solarno was saving me from myself every time he beat the shit out of me."

Sometime during the last few seconds all of the old resentments started coming up; I was determined now to get into Solarno's apartment if for no other reason than Uncle Roddy didn't want me to. He was having the same effect on me as the old man: The more he didn't like what I was doing, the more determined I was to do it.

"And who's supposed to save me every time I see Myra lying there with her throat cut?" I asked him.

There was the threat of thunder in his deep voice. "The bottom line, Neal, is that there's still an investigation going on, and I can't give you permission to go over and poke around at the site of it."

"Then you come with me."

It's hard to say whether I won this contest because he pitied me, or wanted to get rid of me, or on the strength of my own will. Maybe it was just because I could keep my eyes opened wider while we stared at each other. But finally he muttered an obscenity under his breath, got up and came around his desk. He jerked his head in the direction of the door.

We made the short drive over to Bourbon in silence. While he figured out which of the keys went to which of the locks on the outer door, I stole a good look across the street. Mr. D.'s was still closed, but I thought the clothes on the rod were arranged a little differently. Maybe there were more of them, though the bulk of

them had not been pulled off sentry duty in front of the green
door.

Uncle Roddy preceded me up the stairs. I had noticed when we
left the station that he was walking funny, and that he'd had a
little trouble getting into the car. He was limping slowly up the
stairs now.

"What's with the leg, Uncle Roddy?"

"Damned arthritis," he said. "Fluid on the knee. I'm supposed
to stay off it for three days. Imagine that. Mardi Gras, and I'm
supposed to stay off the leg for three days." He wheezed (his
humorless laugh), then started fingering the keys.

There were two more locks on this door.

"He had himself barricaded in like an old lady," I said. "Is there
another door to the place?"

"Nope. No forced entry. He opened the door to whoever killed
him." He flipped the bolt on the second lock and pushed the door
open, standing off to the side so I could go in first.

I stopped dead in the doorway. Directly across the front room,
hung above an overstuffed sofa, was a collection of ten or twelve
tribal masks, each savage face intent upon me, forbidding me.
Any one of them would have been arresting, the eyeless sockets
alive and staring because of the brutal markings around them, but
as a group they had a power of intimidation, ominous and evil,
foreboding death. I was convinced that only a thoroughly evil
man like Solarno could have lived with their daily presence.

"That musta been where they got the idea," Uncle Roddy said
behind me. "That's about what he looked like when they finished
with him, just messier."

"They?" I asked and walked on into the room.

"It wouldof taken more than one person to hold him. Whoever
did the knifework on his face did a precision job, and there was
nothin' in him, no sedative, nothin' like that. Just some tamales
and hot dogs that he ripped in half wit' his teeth and swallowed
wit'out chewing much, like a starving dog stuffin' his gut as fast as
he can wit' any garbage he finds on the street." I assumed he was

quoting the disgusting pathologist. "He was filleted in there," he said, leading the way into a back room.

I didn't understand his use of the word "fillet" until he gave me the graphics, and what he told me made what the pathologist said sound like Chef Paul Prudhomme explaining how to prepare blackened redfish.

The room smelled like vomit. It was set up as an office, with a metal desk and another long table, but it didn't look like a place where any office work got done. It was more of a junk room, too much clutter on the desk to work on it, stacks of *Hustler*, *Penthouse* and other skin-trade magazines on the table top. Under the table were boxes of household items, kitchen utensils, light bulbs, those kind of things, that looked as if they'd been sitting there since Solarno had moved in, never needed, so never unpacked. At a glance, there didn't seem to be anything particularly remarkable about the junk. There wasn't even that much of it. The middle of the room was clear except for a huge bloodstain on the carpet and the outline of Solarno's spread-eagle body. They'd strung him between the desk and the table. The table, Uncle Roddy explained, had been moved out of its position against the wall so they could tie his wrists to its legs, his ankles bound in the same way to the desk legs. Then they'd started carving him with a fillet knife, making pairs of blunt triangles, symmetrical, like the tribal mask markings, at the sides of his mouth, nose and eyes. The skin inside the triangles had been peeled away from the bone, cut out around the mouth, and discarded at the side of his body. Someone had vomited in a corner of the room.

As Uncle Roddy talked, I began to feel nauseated myself, and a little faint, with images of Solarno's face swimming in front of my eyes. I saw the killer's face, too, swathed in its own sinister mask of black and purple face paint. I closed my eyes and it floated for a few seconds inside my eyelids, the face of the boy in the police station.

Uncle Roddy was giving me the rest of it, the fillet knife in the bathroom sink, the time of the face carving, the time of death by multiple stab wounds, the anonymous phone call to the police, while I tried to maintain my equilibrium.

I went back into the living room, looking for a place to sit, but I couldn't stay in there with those masks. I sort of reeled across the room, heading for the door to the bedroom, but when I got in there the only place to sit was on the bed, and I couldn't do it, not on the rumpled, messy-looking sheets. I finally backed up and leaned against the doorjamb, hung there really, to wait for the sickness to pass.

Uncle Roddy was right on top of me. "You all right?"

"It's the worst thing I ever heard."

"It's the worst thing I ever saw."

The room stopped sloping at such a peculiar angle. "Could you tell if they took anything?" I asked. "Did they look around?"

"Yeah, they looked around. There were a coupla valuable things they couldof taken but didn't bother to. Why do you ask?"

"Because I'd rather think about that than what you just told me."

He walked past me and flipped on the bedroom light. "I think they took some films," he said.

That piece of information gave me back my strength. Solarno had told Richard Cotton he had something to show him.

Next to the bed, where I hadn't seen it until I went past the door, was a small side table with a movie projector on it. The bed faced a blank white wall.

"Apparently Solarno titillated himself wit' porno movies before he went to bed," Uncle Roddy said.

Well, that sounded like Solarno, but I wanted to know how he knew.

"We found a piece of one. It musta come off the one they ripped outta the projector," he told me.

"A little home entertainment, or was Solarno still into big vice operations?" I asked, examining the projector.

"That's what the vice boys tell me." He shrugged. "Old dogs don't learn new tricks."

"They have anything on him?"

"Not my department, Neal." Translate that: None of your business.

I went to the other side of the bed where there was a dresser. On top of it in a Royal Sonesta ashtray was a Rolex watch and a pair of gold cufflinks. "Some good vice busts could help make Mr. Callahan's office look better right now," I remarked with my back to him.

He didn't answer. I wasn't going to get any information about Solarno's vice activities.

I opened the top drawer of the dresser. Inside was a cigar box. And inside that was a gold star with a diamond on one of its points. I had given the star to Myra for Christmas one year.

There was still some fingerprint powder on it. I turned it over and wiped the dust off our initials.

It could have happened yesterday: We were strolling down Canal Street the week before Christmas when Myra spotted the star in a jeweler's window. I could hear her exclamations about how pretty it was, how much she liked it, dropping enough hints that I would have had to be retarded not to get them. She'd never taken it off while she was alive. The little gold loop it had hung from was still on it; the broken chain had been found next to her bed.

Uncle Roddy came up beside me. "What is it?"

I held it out to him in the palm of my hand. "I gave it to Myra." I gave it to her, and not long afterward, she died.

He stood there looking at it, looking at me. "Go on," he said. "Take it."

"No." I tossed it back in the cigar box. "He took it." And he died, too.

When we got downstairs, Mr. D.'s was open. I could see a man moving behind the counter, but I didn't want to look too hard.

I stopped in front of the district headquarters, but Uncle Roddy just sat there, his eyes fixed on my face.

"He got his, Neal," he said.

I nodded. "Do me another favor, will you, Uncle Roddy? Don't mention any of this to Dad."

He peered out from under those eyelids at me, then he hoisted himself and his bad leg out of the car. I knew he'd get on the phone as soon as he got upstairs.

13

My Ticket
to the Action

I bolted back over to Bourbon Street, but I was too late. Mr. D.'s was locked up tight again. I was beginning to get the idea that the only way to catch up with Mr. D. was to stake out the laundry. But now was not the time, since Mr. D. had already come and gone. And, anyway, there was someone else I wanted to talk to besides Danny Dideaux.

It was almost four-thirty, about the time I usually packed it in for the day and headed over to Lee's office. But when I'd talked to Lee on the phone that morning, she'd told me not to come to the office, but to meet her at her place at eight o'clock. So I had time to kill, and I wanted to kill some of it with Chance Callahan.

I started driving over to Tulane Avenue and South White Street, which wasn't far from where I was, but the traffic was snarled with everybody trying to get to where they had to go before streets were blocked off for the parade that night. I parked and was going through the office door at ten minutes of five. Callahan's secretary was locking up her desk.

I told her who I was, and she said, "It's Mardi Gras, Mr. Rafferty, and we're all trying to get out of here, including Mr. Callahan. Why don't you call tomorrow and let me set up an appointment for you." When you tell them you're a private investigator, they don't exactly consider you a mover and shaker.

I put on what I hoped was a persuasive smile, and asked her if she wouldn't mind just letting him know I was here.

She sighed. "You'll have to tell me what it's in reference to."

I told her it was in reference to Marty Solarno, my ticket to the action these days.

She got a peculiar expression on her face (Was I dangerous? Would she never be rid of Marty Solarno?) and got on the phone to the inner sanctum. She tonelessly stated my name, my business and why I was there, then told me one of the assistant district attorneys would be with me in a moment, and left.

I waited for about five minutes before a young man, mid-twenties, came out of Callahan's office. He was very clean-cut, dressed in a green LaCoste sweater over his striped tie, khaki pants and penny loafers. His round tortoiseshell glasses made him appear studious and serious, but under the glasses was a nose that had been broken a couple of times, and under the alligator on his sweater were a pair of well developed pectorals. A tough guy disguised as Clark Kent gone preppy.

He smiled a tight smile. "I'm Leonard Yastovich, Mr. Rafferty." He shook my hand briefly and weakly. "Mr. Callahan is tied up right now, and he has an early engagement tonight." His voice was strong but low, and more sympathetic than apologetic. I could have been talking to the director of a funeral home. "Of course, he's very interested in any information you might have about Marty Solarno, but he'd appreciate it if you would talk to me about it first."

"I don't think so, Mr. Yastovich. It's nothing personal, you understand, but what I have to say is for Callahan's ears only." I couldn't very well tell him I was there to get information, not give it.

His mouth struggled to smile. "I'm sorry, then." His shoulders lifted and one hand came toward me, palm up—a gesture of apology. Or maybe it was supplication, because he started to say something else.

I cut him off. "Don't be. Callahan can figure out how to let me know if he wants to talk to me." I left Leonard Yastovich with his mouth puckered and his palm still out, a tough playing the part of an uptight collegiate panhandler who'd failed to get the money from the last passerby.

I pulled up behind the brown Olds at the side of Lee's apartment just before eight o'clock. I noticed on the way to the front door that the bags of groceries were gone. So was the Mustang; she wasn't home yet.

I got back in my car, and rolled the window down halfway so I could smoke. It was a nice night, with the weather warming up, a trend the weathermen said would continue through Mardi Gras. Thoughts and images twirled lazily in my head like the smoke from my cigarette twirling lazily out the car window. Nothing was disturbing, not even Marty Solarno. What was past would stay put; what was coming would come. I was calmer than I'd been all day, and content, waiting for Lee. I gazed drowsily at the clock on the dashboard. But as the minute hand went round and round and nothing happened, the drowsiness began to go, and the wires inside wound tighter and tighter. Then I was wide awake with the kinds of thoughts I'd been thinking for so long that they'd become as much a part of the way I functioned as eating or going to the bathroom.

It was a way of freely associating everything in my life with everything else, making connections where connections should never have been made so that each part could be fitted into the whole. It was one part superstition and an equal part of absurd belief that there was no such thing as coincidence. Finding Myra's star provided me with an answer I'd been after for a long time, which should have helped put the whole thing behind me, but instead Myra's death was still with me, in a different way, as something that had come between Lee and me.

This was crazy—Lee knew nothing about Myra. I decided that if I couldn't forget about it, I should tell Lee about it—Angelesi, Myra, Solarno—so that at least she would understand the cause of my preoccupation with the past. Maybe I was more afraid of my own anger than of her reaction. I accepted the truth: She was much calmer and more rational than I was. I resolved to tell her as soon as she got home.

But she didn't get home; by nine-fifteen, I decided I'd been stood up.

As soon as I got to the Euclid, I called Richard Cotton's house. There had been no answer earlier, but this time Paula Cotton answered. She informed me coldly that Richard was at a Sewerage and Water Board meeting, and that she didn't know when he'd be home because after these meetings he usually went with his clients to the Bucktown Tavern. When I asked her who his clients were, she responded as if she were talking to the town idiot, but she told me something I hadn't known before. Richard Cotton was representing the Bucktown residents in the city's suit to move them out of Bucktown and dredge what was their backyard, the Seventeenth Street Canal. The Bucktown residents are an unpopular minority since several hundred houses in uptown New Orleans flood if five inches of rain fall within an hour or two, and there are less than ten structures, not counting the boat sheds, on the canal at Bucktown.

The Bucktown Tavern is a restaurant that isn't really in Bucktown at all. It's across the canal from Bucktown where a pedestrian bridge makes accessible a semicircle of restaurants and lounges on Lake Pontchartrain without going all the way around several acres of condominiums, suburbs and high rises. I hadn't been to any of those establishments for many years, but when I got off the phone I was nagged by the memory that the Bucktown Tavern had come up recently, and I couldn't remember where or in what context.

I spent the next half hour calling Lee's number and Mr. D.'s Laundry so many times that the sequence of tones replayed in my mind the rest of the night like an unwanted melody. I could feel myself getting wired with the aggravation of waiting, so I decided to go to the Bucktown Tavern and talk to Richard.

It was after ten o'clock when I got out to the lakefront. This time of night, in the middle of the week, it wasn't too crowded. I parked across the street from the tavern, alongside West End Park, which runs the length of a long finger into the lake and is surrounded by boathouses that look like corrugated garages, one butted up against the other. Around the end of the park, to the left, is the Southern Yacht Club and marina. In the breeze coming off the lake I could hear the musical cling-clang of rigging against the masts of the sailboats.

Inside the tavern was the clink-clank of silverware as tables were being cleared and set up for the next day. There were still several tables of diners left in the barnlike restaurant. I didn't see Richard at any of them. All around the dining room were mounted trophies of seafood catches (a blue crab with an eighteen-inch spread from claw to claw, a five-foot swordfish) and signs advertising beer. It was a casual, homey place that had a reputation for excellent fresh seafood.

I stayed in the front part where there was a huge dark mahogany bar. No one sat at it, but a waitress stood at one end and hollered at the bartender to fill a couple (pitchers of beer). The hostess came through a swinging door from the kitchen, yelled something else to the bartender, and told me as she pounded the hardwood floor across the room that she was sorry, they stopped taking food orders at ten. All this noise and everybody hollering at everybody else is part of the atmosphere at a New Orleans seafood restaurant. I told her I wasn't there to eat, but asked her if Richard Cotton was. She said he was in the back (she meant a private room) and that he and his party had just been served dinner. I asked her to let him know I was here, but not to hurry, I would wait outside.

It's rare that I'll choose Mother Nature over a drink, but there was a rare quality to the night. I went back through the double entrance doors, down the long walkway that goes over rocks and water, and jumped off when it cleared the rocks edging the lake. I walked out a bit, away from the tavern, so I could see how far the building sat out in the lake on its pilings. It was built so that it angled into the semicircle of neighboring structures, the first or the last, depending on which side of the crescent you started. I could see stretched along the back side of the restaurant a dock that boats could tie up to while the owners went in for a snack.

The lake was black and shiny under the star-shot sky, moving placidly with the breeze. I took a deep breath and filled up with brackish air. I went down closer to the rocks, the lake's moisture clinging to my face. A car passed and lit up the jagged edges of the rocks for a few moments. After the sound of it died away, I could hear only the singing masts, and the leaves of the trees in the park brushing one another, and the water lapping at the rocks like a large, soft tongue. I stood in the grip of these sounds, facing the endless expanse of water, not really thinking, just absorbing, not quite content, feeling that Mother Nature wasn't either. It was an eerie spell she cast on a clear, early-spring night. Fresh and new and volatile.

The throbbing engine of a Lafitte skiff moving in slowly from the east broke the spell. They're called Lafitte skiffs because the first design came from across the river in Lafitte. Down that way they would be flat-bottomed for easier maneuvering in the shallow bayous. This was a small one, about thirty feet, but round-bottomed for stability in deeper water, its unique broad-in-the-middle, skifflike shape outfitted for trawling. A davit for the net curved out over the fantail that juts off the stern of all Lafitte skiffs. But it was too early in the year for shrimping, which is what the skiffs are chiefly used for, and I didn't see any nets, or lines, or trawl boards. I could see two men silhouetted on the deck, though, as the boat slid over the black-glass water of the lake to the dock of the tavern.

One of the men jumped onto the dock and secured the skiff. His white rubber boots immediately identified him as a fisherman. The other man began handing him large baskets, the kind the fishermen put crabs in as they empty their traps. These men and many others like them were probably putting in extra time and running extra traps out in the lake in preparation for the long Mardi Gras weekend ahead when locals and out-of-towners alike would flock out here to eat the spicy boiled seafood that can't be found anywhere else but New Orleans.

The two men moved with calm, unhurried efficiency. While the one on the dock moved the baskets inside the restaurant, the other got a hose and began washing down the skiff. I watched them, wondering what it was about the Bucktown Tavern I couldn't remember.

Behind me, I heard Richard call my name, and turned to see him jump down from the walkway. He came toward me, hands in his pockets, his shoulders hunched against the chill in the breeze. I told him I hoped I hadn't interrupted anything.

"Just a little beer drinking," he said. I took out a pack of smokes and offered him one. He cupped his hands around my lighter, inhaled and seemed to warm up, relaxing his shoulders. "They'll be at it half the night—my Bucktown clients. You're more than welcome to join us."

"Bunch of Yahoos," I said. "Plenty of those where I come from."

His thin lips curved into a smile. "Yahooism is a state of mind. I enjoy the hell out of those guys. Every time I drink beer with them, my repertoire of dirty jokes doubles."

"Yeah, but who do you get to practice on?"

"Anyone I know in the oil industry, a few lushes I know uptown, and, of course, my law partners, who have no choice but to grin and bear it. The clerks are required to laugh. It's on the application form."

We were both looking out at the water, at the skiff, indulging in a kind of banter we used with each other mostly when we were on the phone, when we weren't talking about serious things like my following his wife or his political ambitions. I took a sidelong glance at him now to see if his face was as deadpan as his delivery, but he was still wearing that slim smile.

The man hosing the skiff threw the hose back on the dock, revved up the engine, and took off as soon as his partner hit the deck. We watched until they were out of sight, going around a thin slice of land bordering the marina, the end of which is called The Point and is a famous make-out place for teenagers.

Getting back to dirty jokes, I had one for Richard, but this one wasn't too funny. So I filled him in on Solarno's murder, without getting too graphic, and mentioned that it appeared that nothing other than a film had been taken from the apartment.

He jumped right on that, turning into the wind to look at me, his longish blond hair blowing across his forehead. "He said he had something to show me. Do you think it was a film? God, that would be almost too much to hope for."

"I thought of that," I told him, "but it wasn't the film that was in his projector because the piece of it that was left had a couple of frames of skin on it."

He frowned and smoothed his hair back, out of his eyes. "But someone bothered to take that film and whatever other films may have been there."

"I thought of that, too. Who else would Solarno tell if he had something?"

"How would I know?" he asked impatiently, tossing his head, seeming irritated with the breeze, which kept blowing his hair around.

"Well, he had to tell someone else besides you, assuming taking the film was no coincidence."

"But he didn't tell me that what he had was a film." He jammed his hands in his pockets and found an angle more compatible with the wind.

"Doesn't mean he didn't tell someone else. There's not too much else to go on."

"I realize that." More conciliatory now. "I take it that means you're not ready to quit."

"No, I'm following a couple of things"—I didn't mention Mr. D.—"long shots." He nodded, but like he wasn't so sure. "I went to Callahan's office today," I went on. "I didn't get past the prep-school alligators in his moat."

"What did you do that for?" This was not mere impatience. He was irritated. With me.

"Because there's not much else to do. Because talking to Callahan might stir up the pot. Because I'll do almost anything for some action these days."

I didn't get the desired reaction, which was a laugh. Instead he turned to the lake again and did some of the kind of thinking he's good at doing while you hang on the phone.

"Okay," he said finally, "then put on a black tie and come to a pre-ball cocktail party at my house tomorrow night. Callahan's supposed to make an appearance."

I expressed surprise at the two opponents' socializing, and doubt that Callahan would show.

"It's a crossing-of-the-swords gesture," Richard said. "He'll show."

Never during the course of our conversation did he ask if I'd found out anything about Myra. And since he didn't ask, I didn't tell him.

When I got home I played the unchained melody on the phone a few more times before I gave up on Lee for the night. I was standing in the bedroom stripped down to the skivvies when there was a hard, curt rap on the front door. This particular knock was distinct; I'd gotten to know it well late last summer.

I didn't figure anyone would expect me to be dressed at this time of night. I looked for my robe on the back of the bathroom door, but only Lee's blue-flowered kimono with an occasional dragon head popping out of the foliage was there. I slipped it on, my arm going through the opening at the armpit, a design feature I truly appreciated when the kimono was on Lee. I wrestled my way out of the armpit opening and into the sleeve, which was big enough for two of my arms, making progress toward the door, but not fast enough for his impatient knuckles. I secured the sash at the waist and flung open the door, almost getting the set of knockers in my face.

"Come in, Lieutenant," I said, backing away. "Sergeant." They both walked past me without a greeting. Uncle Roddy did some heavy breathing as he let himself down into a chair at the dinette table. Fonte waited until his superior was comfortable, then sat. I stood over the two of them. "Gee, what fun. We haven't done this for a long time." I sort of sashayed into the kitchen, the kimono, which was ankle length on Lee, flapping at my calves. I brought back the bottle of Scotch and three glasses. Uncle Roddy didn't seem to notice my colorful garb, but Fonte was giving me a peculiar look, and he had stopped chewing his gum.

I poured Scotch for all. Uncle Roddy drained his three fingers' worth and held his glass out for more. He didn't look so good.

"Wanna put the leg up, Lieutenant?" I started moving the extra chair into position for him.

"No, no," he said, annoyed. "Just tell me what I wanna know so I can get outta here."

"I'll do my best."

I would have expected a jab from Fonte by now, but he had managed to tear his eyes away from me to seek out the possibilities of the bedroom. The bedroom door, however, was only half open.

"I get the feeling you're interested in Marty Solarno for reasons other than personal," Uncle Roddy said.

"Any interest I have in Solarno ends up being personal."

"Don't try to get clever wit' me, Neal." His mood was foul.

"That's not being clever; that's the truth," I said.

"Is it still the truth, even after today? Aren't you satisfied about Myra Ledet now?"

He was being a lot nastier than I thought the occasion called for. Not only that, but I didn't like the idea of talking about Myra in front of Fonte. Fonte, however, did not seem to be interested in the lieutenant and me, but in setting a new world's record for silence, and craning his neck to get a better view of the bedroom. He jerked his head at it. "Bathroom back there?" he demanded.

The kimono sleeve dusted the table as I made a gesture for Fonte to have at it. I regarded Uncle Roddy with a cocked head and a slightly curled lip while I waited for Fonte to find his way to relieve himself or satisfy himself, or whatever.

I told Uncle Roddy, "I don't ever expect to be *satisfied* about Myra, but whether *you* like the way I'm going about it or not, I *am* trying to put it all behind me."

"Okay, Neal. You don't have to be so touchy. I just wanna know who's got you messin' around in the Solarno murder."

I let my mouth gape wide at him. "Uncle Roddy, I told you

why I wanted to go into Solarno's apartment. What makes you think there was any other reason? Wasn't that reason enough?"

His eyes drooped lazily, and he flapped one of his big mitts at me. "Sure, sure. First you wanna know if they took anything outta Solarno's apartment. Then you show a lotta interest in the movie projector. Nex' thing, you're askin' me about Solarno's vice activities when you *know* Solarno always had some operation goin' on. I don't figure you'd be all that interested in what Solarno was into if all you're worried about is Myra Ledet. Then you cap it off wit' a remark about Chance Callahan's office and vice busts. I ain't stupid, Neal."

I rested the fingertips of both hands against my chest, copying one of his favorite gestures. "I can't be interested in the man who murdered Myra?" My voice nearly cracked with disbelief. I cleared my throat. "Once a cop, always a cop, Uncle Roddy."

There was this small, nasty smile on his lips. He reached over and fingered the kimono. "I also know you're practically livin' wit' the Diamond woman. I figure that must go a long way toward easin' your burden."

I sat back, out of his reach, and matched his smile. "So it does." Fonte came back from the bathroom. "I hope you found everything to your satisfaction, Sergeant."

He reached for the bottle with a grunt of disgust, probably annoyed that Lee wasn't stretched out nude on the bed.

"So what does Richard Cotton think Solarno had on him?" Uncle Roddy shot at me.

"I have no idea," I answered truthfully.

"Do you have any knowledge that your client is involved in any sort of vice operation, crime against nature, et cetera?"

"Which client is that, Lieutenant?"

"Cotton!" The name erupted from his craterlike mouth.

"Richard Cotton is frequently a client of mine, but he doesn't happen to be right now." After all, no money had exchanged hands, nor was it going to.

"Well, I don't like the way he comes pussyfootin' around the police station, and I don't believe for one minute he don't know who this guy is who lets himself into his house and burns up in his fireplace. I figure he's lucky we don't have the time to investigate dead junkies. If he thinks his name or his money or his perfect smile turns everything he says into the truth, he's wrong."

This last gave me a good idea of the problems Richard was going to have running for political office in a city like New Orleans.

Uncle Roddy hauled himself laboriously to his feet, and added a postscript. "In my book, he's a liar and a murder suspect, and at that I may be tellin' you what's good about 'im."

I opened the door for him, and watched him limp down the hallway. Fonte started after him, then turned around suddenly, a look of puzzlement on his face. He came the few steps back toward me.

"Listen," he said, "do you always dress like that when you're alone?" His head and shoulders jerked, seeming to bring a snort of laughter up out of him. He turned and went back down the hallway, his gum pops audible until the elevator carried them away.

14

Mr. D.'s Laundry

It was eight-thirty the next morning before I talked to Lee. As worried as I'd been, when I heard her voice what I felt was irritation.

"Where have you been?" I wanted to know. I was cross because the woman at her answering service was in the process of telling me that Ms. Diamond had already called for her messages when Lee picked up the phone.

"Sleeping," she said.

"Where?" All I meant by that was had she been at home or at the office.

There was, however, what you could call a pregnant pause before she answered shortly, "Here," meaning at her office.

"Hey," I said, trying to be light, "I'm the one who got stood up."

"And I am sorry, which I would have said to begin with, but I wasn't given half a chance."

"True. So what happened?"

"I had a tail. I didn't get in until almost four. I decided to sleep here because I have an appointment at nine."

"You still could've called."

"No, I couldn't; I was too tired. Come on, Neal, do we have to go through the whole routine?"

"Well just excuse me all to hell."

"Neal, please. We both know more or less what each other is

92

doing. We both know about the risks we take. Can't we just be glad to hear from each other and feel relief privately?"

"I'm an emotional guy, but, okay, we'll do it your way and feel good about acting so grown-up."

"Don't get me wrong," she said, "I'm glad to know you worry about me, but hearing about it makes me feel—I don't know—queasy."

I held the phone away from my ear and made some faces at it, then I said, chipper as all hell, "Well, we can't have that, can we? I'd rather show you how relieved I am, anyway. How about tonight—wanna go out?" I started to tell her about Richard Cotton's party, but she was too fast.

"I can't. I've got a job, and then I need to go home and get a good night's sleep."

As if she couldn't get one with me there. Well, there was probably something to that, but I didn't feel any warmth coming from her, no indication that it would make her glad to see me sometime. Instead, I got the impression she was anxious to get off the phone. So I got off.

The next person I had to tackle, I thought without any joy, was Mr. D. There was nothing to do but go stand around on Bourbon Street until he showed. I looked at my watch. Quarter to nine. No rush to get over there. I thought morosely about Lucky Dogs (the vendors sell them out of carts shaped like an enormous hot dog in a bun) and hot tamales, Marty Solarno's last meal. Of course, there was always corn on the cob. But people on the street eating corn on the cob seemed to stand out in a crowd. I guess it's the boredom—I get ravenous on a stakeout.

Most laundries and dry cleaners are open early, not that Mr. D.'s was like most. But since I knew the number so well, I gave it a try. I nearly forgot what I was going to say when a man answered on the first ring, "Mr. D.'s Laundry." His voice had that New Orleans nasal quality that, for some reason, seems most prevalent out in Jefferson Parish, though I'm sure that's my own personal bias. The best way I know to describe it is to say that it sounds like

Brando's Godfather, except that the Godfather had a huskiness in his throat, as if he had some physical difficulty speaking. In New Orleans the nasalness just sounds like laziness.

I slipped over into a lazier speech pattern myself. "Mr. D.? Been tough to find you open. If you gonna be there awhile, I'm on the way."

"Who's on the way?"

"Name's Rafferty?"

"Who sent you?"

This was the question I'd been trying to avoid. "No one. I'm bringin' some clothes."

"Look, pal, I do custom cleaning here, pickup and delivery, no off-the-street trade. I gotta full loada customers."

"I gotta reference."

"Who might that be?"

I knew it was wrong before I said it. "Marty Solarno."

"Not good enough." He hung up.

I grabbed my coat and literally ran the two blocks across Canal Street, and the four blocks into the French Quarter. I knew he would beat me, but I had to try.

I had played Mr. D. wrong. It was no consolation to think I would have been here anyway, standing on Bourbon Street on a damp and dismal day in February, amidst the ammonia and disinfectant smells over the food and garbage smells, all of which, though, worked well as an appetite suppressant.

It was over seven hours later that a man in a black leather sports coat stopped in front of the door to the laundry and put a key in the padlock. Although it wasn't that cold—the temperature was in the sixties—the dampness made it feel much colder. My feet felt wet and they hurt as they rubbed inside my shoes. My ankles creaked when I walked across the street.

Mr. D. wasn't as old as he'd sounded on the phone. He was pushing thirty, but not hard. He was about five eleven and thin, but not weak looking. His shoulders were broad and his hands had that long, sinewy look; I guessed his leather-clad arms did, too. But he wasn't anything to worry about. I didn't, however, want to have to strong-arm Mr. D. He probably had more friends on Bourbon Street than I did in the rest of the city, and I doubted that they occupied themselves all day making five-dollar bets on friendly games of pool, or practicing law (not in a courtroom, anyway).

As soon as I opened the door, he looked up from a plastic container of what appeared to be laundry slips and grinned at me. His grin was like his head, wide and boxy.

"Mr. Rafferty, I presume," he said, good-natured as hell, friendly as a used car salesman.

"Okay," I said. "I give up."

"Seven hours don' make you parta the masonry, pal."

I suppose that everyone I'd seen come out of his business establishment with a broom that day was part of a network of spies.

"So what can I really do for you, Rafferty?"

"I'm interested in some films."

"Well, there's no harm in that, is there? You coulda said so to begin wit'."

This Mr. D. was so streetwise that he was making me feel like I had scrambled eggs for brains instead of breakfast. The thing is, in Orleans Parish you can't just walk into a store or video rental place and buy, rent or view pornographic films or tapes anymore, even though showing, selling or renting them is not necessarily illegal unless they can be determined to be obscene under the obscenity law. This may seem confusing, but what it means is that if there is no penetration or ejaculation by the male, which is clearly termed hard-core, what is obscene is left to a judge's discretion. This discretionary law got rid of the peep shows and glory holes. Of course, there are other illegal activities generally associated with the porn industry, like pimping and prostitution and drugs, but I'd like to see the law that can get rid of those. Anyway, I had to credit myself with not being sleazeball enough to know how to play a purveyor to the more esoteric of sexual appetites.

He came around the counter to activate a photoelectric sensor so a buzz would sound if anyone opened the door.

"I rent three shorts, sixty dollars for three days; five for seventy-five. Feature films are more." He turned and gave me some swift eyebrow action. "How 'bout your own double bill—*Devil in Miss Jones* and *Deep Throat?*"

I told him I thought the shorts. He parted the clothes in front of the green door, opened the door, and waited for me to go through first.

It wasn't a big room unless you compared it to the room out front, but it was big enough to hold an extremely antiquated dry cleaning machine, an ironing board, iron on top, a large movable clothes rack stuffed with a variety of dress-up togs including lots of leather and Frederick's of Hollywood–type lingerie, a movie projector and screen, and a bed. The bed was over in the corner of the room guarded by a couple of silver lights on tripods. On a table next to it was a super-eight movie camera. The bathroom was a toilet and sink in a cubicle; the door was a curtain that was now pushed back. There was a back door exit with a long sliding bolt, and black cloth was tacked over the two windows. It was a perfect nook for Mr. D.'s purposes.

"What are you into—hetero; gay; ménage à trois, both ways; S and M; B and D; pintos . . . It's your first time—I'll give you a sample," he offered. Generous guy.

I went for the pintos—live and learn is my motto.

He pulled a straightback chair to the side of the projector for me, and started going through the cans of film stacked on the shelves of the projector stand.

While he found my thrill, I gave him a good once-over. He had a professional, clean-cut hair style. There were some bad pock-marks on his face, but his skin wasn't oily or slimy, and his teeth were white and regular. He had on a polyester shirt, jungle-print motif, not my taste but not horrible either, under the supple, well-cut leather coat. The pants were well cut, too. And he certainly was friendly, a rectangular smile always on his face, and very polite, but there was still something sleazy about him. I guess it could have been the lagoon-scum-green alligator shoes.

He threaded the film and a Southern belle decked out like

Scarlett O'Hara in a taffeta dress, her hair in coils, was up on the screen. She was in a white, bare room; it could have been this one. There was no sound, but from the faraway look in her eyes and the way she was moping around and kissing the picture of some Rhett type, I got the idea. She sat on the side of a bed done in white ruffles and frills, closed her eyes and ran her tongue all around her red, red lips so you could tell she was going into some kind of ecstasy. Next thing, she hikes up the dress, under which she has on only a garter belt and black fishnet stockings, and begins to masturbate. Someone must enter the room, because suddenly she sits up with terror on her face. The camera pans slowly to a big black buck wearing a tuxedo jacket over leather pants with the crotch cut out of them. He's carrying a whip.

I lost some of the continuity at this point because I realized with a start that I was supposed to go to Richard Cotton's party in a couple of hours, and the last time I'd pulled out my tux I'd discovered it was full of tiny holes—the work of some kind of insect that lives in New Orleans' closets. I'd never make it to one of the rental places.

By now the buck has ripped the girl out of her gorgeous dress, tied her to the bed, and is whipping her fiercely, leaving red slashes all over her buttocks and thighs. Her mouth is wide open; she is screaming, but soon her screams turn into defeated whimpers. The film is cut, and in the next scene, the same girl, though it takes you a moment to realize it, has gone through a dramatic transformation. Her hair is down and frizzed all around her head, and when she smiles, you can see that one of her front teeth is dead. She is giving the buck the come-on. She is still wearing nothing but red stripes. They get down to more serious entertainment, but nothing that would be considered hard-core pornography by a judge who has to decide whether or not to issue an arrest warrant.

I'd had enough. I told Mr. D. to can it.

"Not into costume drama?" he asked. I almost choked. "You wanna be more specific about what you like, I got somethin' for everybody here."

"Show me one of Marty Solarno's favorites."

He was very cool. He picked out a film without a look or a comment. It was called *Party Time*. A lot of naked men and women cavorted around doing odd things with even odder accoutrements, like coat hangers and candles, but, again, only soft-core stuff. The girl with the dead front tooth was in this one, too, although it might have been another girl with a dead tooth. I studied the faces of the rest of the actors. There was no one even vaguely familiar. I told Mr. D. that wasn't it either.

"How about some local celebrities?" I requested.

He turned off the projector. "Okay, Rafferty, I got you pegged as some kinda private cop. Whadaya want?"

I didn't want Mr. D. turning mean on me, so I stood up and gave it to him straight. "I want a film that Solarno was anxious to show, only he didn't make it through the night."

He didn't play dumb. "Blackmail?" he asked. "Look, Marty rented films from me, but they were films like you just saw. I get 'em from a New York distributor."

"It looks to me like you go in for some local production." I nodded at the super-eight.

"Sure. We do some skits, for private parties."

"Maybe it was one of those."

"Uh-uh. I keep my operation clean."

"Yeah," I said. "Did you ever loan the camera to Solarno?"

"I can tell you didn' know Marty, pal. I'da never seen it again. I don' know about this film, pal."

There was no use pressing him; he wasn't going to talk no matter what he knew. I said quietly, "I hope not, Mr. D., because I think the film got him killed."

He held up a hand to stop me. "I don' wanna know nothin'."

I started toward the door, but got an idea. I jerked a thumb over my shoulder at the clothes rack. "You got a tuxedo I can rent?"

15

The Party

I held the tuxedo up closer to the light. "Is it clean?" I asked.

Mr. D. wasn't offended. He just smiled wider, his face sharp with right angles. "This is a *clean*ers," he said, his voice so shallow and nasal that he sounded like Peter Lorre.

I thought Chance Callahan might be unfashionably early to avoid those being fashionably late, so I got to Richard Cotton's house on time. Quiro opened the front door.

"Good evening, Quiro."

He was suited up, looking suave and handsome. "Please come in." He didn't call me boss; he didn't act as if he'd ever seen me before. I followed him down the hallway, having to fight an impulse to imitate his smooth, graceful, soundless walk.

The furniture in the double parlor had been rearranged, for openness, not intimacy. In the second parlor, a couple stood in front of the clean, cold fireplace, but I could see the logs burning and the man's legs stretched across the wide hearth, and Lee standing over him.

Quiro took me past them, through the dining room where a lot of elaborate, untouched food was laid out on the table, to a narrow passageway between the dining room and the kitchen where a bartender was stationed. The doorbell sounded, and he left me there.

Paula Cotton came into the passageway from the kitchen side. Her blonde hair was swept up, one shoulder was bare. From the other shoulder a mass of white sequins fell to the floor. She looked like the Snow Queen.

"Mr. Rafferty," she said formally. Her pale pink lips looked uncomfortable and unfriendly pressed together as they were. It seemed to me we had been on a first-name basis once.

"Mrs. Cotton," I answered in kind, dipping my head in a bow.

She ignored the gesture and the irony, issued some fast instructions to the bartender, and left, back through the kitchen.

I returned to the dining room, my lips burning nicely from the first sip of Scotch. I surveyed the food and decided it was too pretty to be appetizing. I escaped from row after row of grinning pink crescents of jumbo shrimp, laid out in such perfect order in their marinade, through another doorway.

I'd never been this far back in the house, which was much larger than you would think from its deceptively narrow front. The room I was in, to the side of the kitchen, was a den, with another large fireplace and a floor of huge marble squares. In front of the fireplace was a bearskin rug. Over the mantel was a deerhead. The room was a deviation from the traditional New Orleans velvet-draped formal front parlor, but it was a standard deviation—the lodge effect. Beyond it was a glassed-in sun porch, white wicker furniture, green plants. Off to the side was the library, a long comfortable sofa, bookshelves over cabinets, the obligatory antique desk and Oriental rug, the rich smell of the books. There was, of course, the odd, spectacular piece of furniture, for instance in the library a glass-fronted art deco cabinet. Each room, the house as a whole, was stamped with a certain look: stylishly comfortable, fashionably conservative, with a few calculated and rich-looking discrepancies in the decor. There were probably four more houses a lot like it in this block alone.

I stayed in the library until I finished my drink—I wasn't in the mood for idle social chitchat. The drink put a dull glaze on everything; my throat felt scratchy. Some payoff for seven hours on cold concrete.

In twenty minutes the party had beefed up considerably, and the front rooms were crowded with people. I stood in the wide doorway that opened into the hallway from the second parlor and scanned the room for Chance Callahan. Richard was standing near the window opposite me talking to several people. His tuxedo looked as if it was made out of cashmere. He was elegant and at home in it, not zoot-suited as I undoubtedly appeared in Mr. D.'s polyester-blend special.

I walked on in so I could see who was in the next room. The dull glaze was broken by rainbows flashing. Paula Cotton passed in front of me to get to a couple standing off to themselves. There were radiant smiles, exclamations, hands extended, kisses exchanged. Boy, did they know how to have a good time.

I watched Paula for a few moments. All of her smiling and kissing and laugh-touched talking seemed very artificial, but because her animation was accompanied by the glitter of white sequins, and because it was directed to other exquisitely dressed people who responded with such pleasure under the gracious high ceilings and crystal chandeliers, it seemed appropriate, and, finally, attractive. The lure of the rich and beautiful. Her alabaster arm moved, the fingers on the hand at the end of it rippled, the heavy rocks rode the third finger and stayed put.

My eyes left the glitz and filmed over again. But just for a few seconds—what they found next was Lee. She was standing in front of the long window I'd thrown the iron chair through, almost perfectly framed by blue velvet curtains except for a man who was talking to her and whose back was to me. I knew she'd spotted me first. Maybe it was that her eyes had flicked back to him just as I saw her. She didn't look at me again until I took a step toward her. Immediately I got warned off with a swift eye flash. The man saw it, too. He started to turn around, but she touched his arm lightly and said something that kept his attention on her.

I moved off to the side where I could see her better. He was talking to her very closely now. Her head was bent so that her hair, not elaborately done, but softly curling around her face as

always, grazed his chin every now and then as he spoke. He
flipped a hand after making a statement, rhetorical perhaps, and
then the hand landed on her forearm. Then on her shoulder. Now
it was grasping her elbow. He was awfully touchy. And I was
awfully jealous, thinking who wouldn't want to touch her. There
wasn't a woman in the room who came close to her, I thought, and
she wasn't decked out in beaded brocade or bugled satin. She
wasn't encased in sequins or dripping with jewels. She had on no
jewelry at all, and her dress was very simple, a black floor-length
tube held up by two round thin straps, but hardly shapeless. The
top was scooped so a hint of cleavage showed. The material
stretched just tight enough across her breasts, and fitted just close
enough to her waist and hips. The material, I also noted, and it
turned up my lips, was a black-on-black design of diamonds. I was
awfully glad to see her.

I got around to noticing that this man she was talking to was
almost as pretty as she was. He had jet-black hair that reflected
the blue of the curtains, and fine smooth skin, and that kind of
bone structure that men in magazine ads have. Those men,
though, don't look like they can talk. They don't look like they
can eat, drink or go to the bathroom. They pose. But this one was
talking a blue streak; he was on a roll, touching and gesturing,
getting closer to Lee, his shoulders hunched forward intimately in
an effeminate way, then backing off, his eyebrows raised expec-
tantly for her reaction. He was very dramatic, and I was beginning
to think he would go on all night. When a uniformed maid passed
with a tray of champagne, I took two.

Because I was thinking he was gay, it didn't occur to me until he
shifted position and seemed to start in on a new subject that
perhaps Lee was with him. The implication of this was that she
had deliberately lied to me and so was through with me. I drained
off one glass of champagne and slid it on a passing tray. But then
she put a hand on him, interrupting him, and said something to
him, dismissing him. She walked slowly across the room to me,
trying not to smile that smile.

She stopped in front of me and put her weight on one hip. I kept my shoulder to the wall I was leaning up against.

"Hey," I said after about an eternity, "wanna go home and stay up all night with me?"

"Yes," she said. She moved a little closer to me. She said something about missing me that was barely audible, but I didn't have to hear her; I was watching her lips bump each other softly.

I got off the wall and straightened up, which put me close enough to her to smell her. One hand was occupied with the glass of champagne; the other hand, with a mind of its own, reached out to her. A rosy tint began to spread across her chest and up her neck. It was the first time, and maybe the only time I was likely to see Lee Diamond flustered. She stepped back and looked to each side guiltily, as if she expected everyone to be able to see the sparks that were flying between us. I half expected it myself.

I said, "I'll see you after the party." I turned away from her with effort and went off to the bar to get a real drink.

Chance Callahan's arrival was the arrival of a celebrity. He was past being fashionably late; he walked in at the peak of the party. I was wrong to think Callahan might try to avoid anybody. He was enjoying his fame. People twisted and craned their necks to get a glimpse of him as he and his entourage made their way into the gathering, shaking hands and waving.

Callahan had that quality called presence shimmering off him like an aura. Part of it had to do with his looks. He had enough of a translucent Irish complexion that his skin glowed without being at all ruddy. His head was sleek and oval, like an egg, the ears set close to it. The rest of his features were clumped together in the middle of his face. His forehead sloped back gently into his hairline, and his one-tone gray hair was combed straight back. It fitted his head like a pewter skullcap. Viewing him in profile, as I was, he looked like a silver seal.

The other part of his presence was his enormous self-confidence and total lack of fear. This was a man who did not need to avoid anybody—ever. He was up to handling anything. He did not worry about anything, either. He had said there would be no riots after the project killings, and there hadn't been. He defied the anger of the black community by refusing to discuss the police shooting of a black youth. I had the feeling he would pull it all out of the bag in plenty of time.

He and Richard toasted each other with champagne and exchanged remarks that had everyone near them laughing and nodding. A couple of women even clapped at one point. But as I watched the two candidates together, I got diverted because I suddenly remembered what it was about the Bucktown Tavern I had forgotten. The tavern was mentioned in the newspaper article I'd read that day at the old man's house while he yapped at me.

When I got my turn, I went up to Callahan and told him who I was. Even though he and I were about the same height, he seemed to be looking down at me. He had on his face that look of complacency people get when everything in their life is going right, and so they think they're superior. I could taste my dislike for him.

"Oh, yes," he said pleasantly, "you're the one who kept saying Mr. Angelesi was a murderer."

He didn't bother to keep his voice down. Anyone who was within hearing distance turned around.

"I'm also the one who was in your office yesterday about Marty Solarno's murder."

The party didn't seem to be so noisy anymore.

Callahan ignored what I said. "You know, there are a lot of people who say that if it hadn't been for you, Mr. Angelesi would still be the district attorney."

What was this—some kind of cloaked way of saying, "Gee, thanks, pal"?

I was ready to go on having two different conversations for as long as it took. "Maybe you already know everything there is to know about Marty Solarno's murder."

At this point, I'll admit I was causing a scene. But Callahan didn't mind; he was still smiling down at me. Before he had a chance to reply, Quiro was in my ear.

"Richard wants to see you in the back, boss."

"Okay." But I wasn't about to get led off by the host's manservant now. I waited for Callahan.

He spoke as much to the crowd as to me. "I know this much: He used to sing anywhere, too." He rocked forward on the balls of his feet when he said "used to," and because he said it like he was telling a joke, people laughed.

I spoke to him quietly so not many could hear. "Seen any interesting movies lately?"

"Please, come." Quiro was in my ear again, but this time he took me by the forearm, and tightly enough that I would have had to scuffle with him not to follow. But I had said everything I wanted to say to Callahan.

Richard and Paula were out in the hallway. Paula's pink lips twitched with anger. I apologized to her, but Quiro kept me moving toward the back of the house.

"He didn't start it," Richard told his wife. She did some angry whispering, and then—I just caught it—Richard said, "Well, if you wouldn't have invited *her*, I wouldn't have invited *him*."

Quiro let me precede him through the dining room. When we got into the den, I said to him, "Private detectives don't seem to be very popular right now."

"Not right now," he agreed. He motioned me to go into the library.

"The worst that can happen is that the party will be the talk of the town."

"You will be the talk of the town, boss."

Richard came up fast and the two of us went into the library. He closed the big sliding double doors behind us.

"Paula is deathly afraid of any kind of unpleasantness," he said.

"There wouldn't have been any unpleasantness."

"I know. Callahan wouldn't have allowed it." He got a cigarette out of a crystal box on the desk.

"Neither would I." I guess I felt a bit defensive.

"Of course not." He fumbled with a book of matches. I took out my lighter and lit his cigarette. "Thanks." He inhaled, his head tilted back. "What was that last you said to him?"

"I asked him if he'd seen any interesting movies lately."

"Oh God." He sort of crumbled onto the edge of the desk.

"Don't be so nervous, Richard. One of the best ways to get information is to give it—selectively."

"I don't like it."

"I can tell. What I don't like is Rankin coming to my place at midnight to ask me what Solarno had on you."

"What?"

"That's right. He's suspicious that I wanted to get into Solarno's apartment for reasons that weren't personal."

"It's all getting so twisted." He rolled the cigarette around in his fingers and took a short, inelegant drag.

"I'm doing my best to untwist it."

He nodded, but without much conviction, and put out his cigarette. "I can't be gone long. A lot of people are going to be leaving for the ball." He got up and started toward the door.

"Richard." He turned around. "Do you remember the kid on the motorcycle who was gunned down by the cops?" He said yes vaguely. He looked distracted and depressed. "He worked at the Bucktown Tavern. Did you know him?"

He stared at me. "No. I've got to go."

Maybe he did know the kid, or maybe he was too much of an aristocrat to notice a busboy.

I went out into the den after he left, but I didn't want to go up front. I figured I'd upset Paula Cotton enough for one night. I waited until I saw Quiro come through the passageway and into the kitchen. I signaled to him. He slid into the den on those cat feet.

"Quiro, would you ask Miss Diamond to come back here?"

"Sure, boss." He did his quick dancerlike movement and floated away to get Lee.

We left through the kitchen. As soon as we got into some shadows at the side of the house, I pulled her to me and kissed her for a long time, willing myself to forget about Solarno and Callahan and the Cottons. But Lee wasn't ready to forget yet.

We were still leaning against each other. My hands were doing laps up and down the length of her back.

"I'm not sure what went on back there, Neal, but is it too strong to say that you accused Callahan of Marty Solarno's murder, and that he threatened to kill you?"

My hands stopped on her hips. I pushed on her so we were standing apart, took her hand, and started down the driveway.

"You put it like that," I said, "it makes me queasy."

16

The Silver Seal

No one even looked at me funny when I walked into the Euclid at nine o'clock the next morning wearing a tuxedo that had spent the night wadded up on the floor. Part of this was because not much looked strange at the Euclid anymore. The other part is that nothing at all looks strange during Mardi Gras.

I changed clothes, took the tuxedo, and went down to the office. The answering service was clear, and Mr. D. didn't answer. I threw the tux up on a file cabinet; if Mr. D. wanted it back, he knew where to find me.

That afternoon, as I walked over to Lee's, was the first of many times during the next few days that I had the sensation there was a colony of crawlers living under the skin on my back. I was walking down Dauphine Street. Normally, it's one of the quieter streets in the French Quarter, but because of Mardi Gras it was busier with pedestrians than usual. If there was someone following me, he would have to be pretty lousy at it for me to spot him in the Mardi Gras crowds. Not that I didn't try. I stopped on the street during a lull in foot traffic and lit a cigarette, listening for any footsteps that stopped behind me. None did. I took a right on Conti and lingered in the doorway of a bar about a half a block down. No one came speeding around the corner. No one passed me up only to wait a little further along the street. After the first day, I thought maybe I was being paranoid. After the next few days, even though I still hadn't spotted anyone, I knew I wasn't.

There wasn't much else going on to keep me on my toes. Right before Mardi Gras everyone gives up trying to get anything done, or else they disappear until afterward. So on the Monday before the big day the only phone calls I'd got were from my mother. The first time she called to find out how many people were going to be at my apartment the next day to watch the parades so she could make enough potato salad, and to tell me to pick up a king cake at the bakery near the Euclid. The second time was to tell me not to pick up the king cake because she and my sister's kids had decided to make one. When the phone rang the third time I figured she was calling to tell me the king cake was a disaster, and to pick one up after all. But it wasn't my mother. It was Chance Callahan telling me to be at his office in an hour.

When I got there everyone was gone except Leonard Yastovich, who watched me closely until Callahan got off the phone. He told me where to sit, giving me his reluctant, puckered smile, then sat across from me at Callahan's secretary's desk. After that we didn't speak. Yastovich had that look about him, in his tight mouth and his wary eyes, of someone who wanted something badly and would do almost anything to get it. It reminded me of Richard asking if I remembered how it was to be young and reckless. But it showed all over Yastovich that he would do whatever anybody told him to do if he thought it would put him ahead. I didn't think he would wise up. What he was best at was being a lackey, yet he wanted to be more than that. He would be used, as I figured Callahan was using him now, and then discarded when he tried to reap the rewards.

Callahan had me wait long enough to show me how eaten up he was with his own importance. In this business, I've gotten used to those types. What they don't realize is that they'd be respected more if they were on time. It seems childishly simple to me.

Once I was inside, though, he started right in, but not curtly or hurriedly. He was his usual relaxed and smiling self. His sleek head was gleaming.

"I hope you haven't been running all over town telling everyone I killed Marty Solarno," he said.

"I get the feeling it wouldn't bother you much if I did."

"Of course it would. You are known to be a very persistent man."

"If you are referring to my accusations against Angelesi, I don't mind telling you that there is a large qualitative difference in my mind between Marty Solarno being murdered and Myra Ledet being murdered."

"In *your* mind."

"What exactly do you mean by that?" I demanded, getting hot that he might be making a slur against Myra.

"In this office, Mr. Rafferty, murder is murder no matter who it is."

"Right."

"I'm curious about you, Rafferty. I'd like to know what it is that drives a man like you."

"And that's why you called me over here? It's probably nothing you could understand."

"Nothing so crass as ambition—am I right? What is it—love, loyalty, ideals?" I was really getting sick of that smile. "Are you working for Richard Cotton?"

"I work for him sometimes."

"Were you working while the rest of us were partying?"

"I'm also his friend," I said.

"I doubt that. Richard Cotton has no friends. He's too selfish and ambitious, too aware of his superior social status. Of course, he's so aristocratic—one of the beautiful people—that it's difficult to see. Unless you've worked with him."

My hands itched to pound the smugness out of his face. "I'm getting tired of this conversation."

"Then let's talk about Christopher Raven."

"What about him?"

"About how a police informant and junkie lets himself into the candidate's house, makes a fire in the candidate's fireplace, and makes himself at home. And how the candidate says he doesn't know him."

"What are you trying to say, Callahan? Is that the kind of stuff you plan to talk about during the campaign?"

"Oh, really, Rafferty. What's wrong with you? The press will talk about Raven. I'm sure I'll be asked to comment. Of course, I would never make a subjective comment. I think what I just said is a fair representation of what happened."

That damned smile. I really felt hot now. "What is this? You called me up here so I could go back and deliver your threats to Richard Cotton? That's what you're doing—you're threatening him."

"Don't get high-handed with me, Rafferty. You're here because I'm doing you a favor. You came in to see me last week, or don't you remember?"

"Yeah, I also remember you weren't interested then. I wonder— was it something I said? Dropping Marty Solarno's name didn't help. So it must have been the bit about the movies. You want to know if I've seen the film, or if I have a print of the film, or if I know if anyone else has a print. Or maybe it isn't a film at all. You aren't sure, are you?"

"*Au contraire*, Mr. Rafferty." There was a nastiness as well as a prissiness I hadn't heard before, but it suited him well, and at least the smile was gone. "I'm quite sure about a great many more things than you are. I'm quite sure that Richard Cotton hired Marty Solarno. And that he thought Solarno had something on me. Then he hired you. And what neither one of you can be sure about is that Solarno didn't have something on Cotton. You're both amateurs trying to play in the major leagues, so just get out of it now. You, Rafferty. Even what you think you know, you don't. I've done you a favor to tell you anything. Now get out of here."

I got up. "I'm sure of one thing, Callahan. You wouldn't have told me to come over here just to do me a favor."

17

Mardi Gras
Madness

What Callahan had said was true enough: I wasn't sure Solarno hadn't had something on Richard. It would have been like him to supply Richard with a film and Callahan with a tape of Richard sounding a lot like a blackmailer. But then, I wasn't one hundred percent positive there was a film.

What perplexed me as much as anything was Callahan saying that I didn't even know what I thought I knew. The truth was that the more I thought about it all, the less sure I was about anything. The way things were stacking up, with what Richard had said about himself, his hiring Solarno, and the kind of questions Uncle Roddy was asking, I was beginning to suspect he had closer ties to the world of vice than his background and life-style would indicate. And what was Callahan trying to say about Raven—that Richard knew him? Or was he just trying to make me believe that just like he was going to try to make everyone in the city believe that? I didn't know, and I wasn't sure I wanted to know. I liked Richard Cotton.

Nevertheless, I tried to call him. We needed to talk, but by that time on Mardi Gras eve his office was closed and there was no answer at his house. He and Paula had probably ducked out of town.

For the moment, there were other things to think about. Lee

and I were going strong again. We were back to where we had been before the rift of the previous week. But I still wanted to tell her about Myra and my past. Until I trusted her with this confidence, I felt we could go no further. But for the time being I decided to let it ride. She was asking no questions, and, anyway, I'm big on timing.

The city was choked with people; it was difficult to get anywhere. People walked in the streets oblivious to traffic. Everywhere we went we either ran into a parade or a tandem of empty floats on the way to the start of one.

The night before Mardi Gras we stayed at my apartment to get ready for the open house I'd had yearly since moving into the Euclid. Besides the fact that it didn't flood, the other good thing about my apartment was that the parades passed right outside my windows. So if you didn't want to be in the crowd, you could watch from upstairs. And when my sister's kids decided they'd caught enough beads they could entertain themselves riding up and down the elevators.

We were up by six o'clock Mardi Gras morning. By seven people were lined up on St. Charles Avenue with ice chests for their beer, ladders for their kids, and lawn chairs for their old folks.

When my mother and sister arrived, Lee and I took the kids and walked down St. Charles, checking out the costumes and watching people get drunk at eight o'clock in the morning. We were close to Lee Circle when the kids spotted the old man and their father. Michael is a cop, and he was working a double shift, as he always does on Mardi Gras, walking up and down the assigned beat on St. Charles Avenue. The old man was having his big fun for the day, walking with Michael and his partner until Zulu, the first parade, rounded the corner at Jackson and St. Charles to head downtown. It's just the past few years that Zulu, the only black carnival crew, has been on an established route. Their floats used to wander all over town, and if you were lucky enough to find them, you might catch one of the prized gilded coconuts they throw—if one didn't hit you on the head first. The old man, talking to me, told us to run along, then, to Lee, said he'd meet us back at the Euclid as soon as Zulu passed.

By the time Rex, the King of Carnival, was in front of the Euclid, the crowds were thick as Irish stew, and Lee had made another friend—Reenie's nine-year-old son, Johnny. He was scrounging for beads, and every pair he caught, he gave to her until she told him that if she wore any more, she'd be bent double. He still showed her everything he caught before he bagged it, though.

I had Kate, the younger one, up on my shoulders. She was protesting that she wasn't catching as much as her brother, but by covering my eyes to hold on to me I was having trouble getting anything for her. My mother was standing next to us bagging Kate's throws and yelling at her to stop putting her hands over Uncle Neal's eyes. One float passed, another one approached, and the crowd surged, pushing us closer. I heard Johnny shout, "Hey, Lee, where ya goin'?" I pulled off one of Kate's little hands in time to see Lee dash out into the street in between two floats that were rolling along at a pretty fast clip. My heart did a double flip, but she made it across and was squeezing into the crowd on the other side, then the second float blocked my view of her.

I swung Kate, screaming and flailing, off my shoulders and told my mother to hang on to her. People shoved me and cursed me, but I made it to the front and got across the avenue, dodging some dukes on prancing horses. I pushed through another barrier of unwilling people until I was on the far side of the neutral ground where I could move unhindered. I walked along the edge of the crowd looking for Lee. I walked for two blocks, but she had disappeared.

My mother and I had to fight to get the kids upstairs. The truck parades follow Rex and go on well into the afternoon. Every truck was a pair of beads or trinket in the day-long competition to see who could catch the most. We let them watch about twenty of them before we herded them back to the apartment. Lee still hadn't returned.

I saw my sister head into the bedroom and followed her. She

was stretching out on the bed, her big stomach making lying down difficult.

"Feeling bad?" I asked.

"Tired," Reenie said. "They've got me afraid to do anything for fear I'll lose this baby."

"It's not long now, is it?"

"Less than two weeks. Neal, will you do me a favor? Will you relieve Ma with the kids for a while, and take me home later?"

"Sure." Her eyes were already closing.

I went out into the living room, closing the door behind me. Lee was back. The old man had her cornered, and was well into one of his acts, talking about the good ol' days. She was a good audience, laughing and asking him questions, and he was enjoying the hell out of himself. And, I have to admit, I was pleased.

I went downstairs, watched another twenty trucks, then told the kids to take an elevator ride. Meanwhile, several hungry and thirsty people had arrived, mostly the old man's friends, among them Uncle Roddy and Fonte. A few more people were heading out, among them some of my friends from Grady's bar. They were on their way back to the bar to hang over the pool tables. Not even Mardi Gras breaks their routine. I walked to the door with them, promising Murphy Zeringue, a longtime friend and one of Grady's regular pool sharks, that I'd come by for a game soon. I headed into the kitchen for a drink. Running my mouth playing host had made me thirsty. The old man came in behind me.

"Fix Rod'rick a Scotch, Neal," he bellowed as if I were standing in the kitchen of the next apartment. He draped an arm over my shoulder, and came in close to my ear. "Looks like you gotta live one there. If I were you, I'd hang on to her for a while."

If he were me. I suppressed a smile. "Yeah? I thought you were against women cops."

He clapped me on the back. "Just for fun, Neal, just for fun. 'Til somethin' better comes along." He left with Rod'rick's drink.

I stood there, my blood at a fast boil. Reenie came to the kitchen doorway.

"Can we go now, Neal?"

"Yeah."

I went out into the small hallway between the living room and the front door. I was going to get Lee to come with us, but Fonte was grinning all over her, his arm straight out, palm on the wall, blocking her in the corner. The old man was barging in on them.

"Let's get out of here," I said to Reenie.

We had to drive through the back streets until we were far enough uptown to get across St. Charles Avenue, then back down to the Channel. I was still hot from the old man's bullying.

"Okay," Reenie said, "what did he do now?"

"Same old shit," I told her. "He's got to put Lee down—and me—even though I can tell he likes the hell out of her." I imitated him. "Don't fool around wit' women cops, Neal."

"You know that's the way he is. Why can't you just do what you want and let him growl?"

"I don't know," I said.

She didn't say anything else until I pulled up in front of the house. She put her hand on my forearm. "As much as anything, Neal, it's the two of you together. You act like he's your rival, but you're a chip off the old block." Her hand lightly patted my forearm before it withdrew. "Don't be mad at me for saying that."

Red Reenie, I thought, recalling the name I'd tortured her with through childhood because of her reddish-brown hair. I guess she'd taken her share of bullying, too.

"I'm not mad," I said. I kissed her on the cheek and watched her waddle into her side of the double.

Reenie was right. There was a lot of the old man in me. I'd tried to be exactly like him for so many years—not so unusual for a lot of kids—that if Myra Ledet hadn't come along, I may never have realized we were two different people.

I'd been gone from the Euclid a good half hour, but Lee, Fonte, and the old man were still laughing in the corner. Uncle Roddy had joined them.

I got into the middle of them and took Lee by the hand. "Please excuse us, gentlemen." I led Lee off to the bedroom and shut the door behind us.

"Where did you go?" she asked.

"I took Reenie home." I pushed her hair away from her face. "And where did you go this morning?"

"I thought I spotted my shadow, from last week, remember?"

"I thought you were on someone."

"No. I told you *I* had a tail. I spent until four o'clock in the morning trying to draw him out."

I didn't like that, but I figured I'd better not say so. "Strange," I said instead. "I've had the feeling someone's been following me, too. I wonder what's going on." My hand slid down her smooth face to her throat. Her eyes fluttered. I bent and kissed her.

At that moment, the bedroom door flew open. "Hey, Lee!" Johnny yelled. He took one look at the two of us standing there, and said, "Well ex-*cuse* me," and slammed the door shut. Lee laughed.

"Look," I said, "I've had enough of this insanity. We're leaving."

"You're leaving your own party?"

"Ha. It's the old man's party." I got her canvas bag out of the closet. "You go first. I'll throw a few things together and meet you downstairs." She went to the door. "And, look," I added. "Don't let Fonte or Johnny or the old man catch you, okay?"

18

Everyone Needs a Vice

"**P**aula Cotton thinks someone's trying to kill her, Neal."
The Mardi Gras revelers were far behind us. Outside Lee's windows was Audubon Park and in it the insect sounds of the country as night falls. We were stretched out on the futon in the bedroom, drinking some kind of aromatic Chinese tea that Lee liked. I would have preferred a drink, but here it was strictly bring your own, which I hadn't, and which I wasn't encouraged to do. We were talking about the terrorization of Paula Cotton— scraping sounds at the outside doors of the Garden District house, doorknobs turning, late night phone calls from a whisperer. The incidents only occurred at night when she was alone, but that didn't make them attempts on her life.

"It sounds to me like someone's trying to scare her."

"And she's afraid," Lee said, "but she thinks it's more than that. She's been afraid since Christopher Raven got into the house."

I wanted to ask her if Paula Cotton thought Richard knew Raven, or if she had any theories about why Raven was in her house, but I also didn't want to tell Lee about my conversation with Callahan until I talked to Richard. If I was going to betray something, I at least wanted to know what it was. I said, "I can understand that, but I still don't see why she thinks someone is trying to kill her."

"She thinks someone wants her out of the way. He tells her over the phone to get out or he'll kill her. She believes him."

"So why doesn't she get out—take a trip?"

"I suggested that, but she says it's running away, she wouldn't know how long to stay, and it would make her angry."

"Why doesn't Quiro come stay with her, instead of staying across the lake?"

"She doesn't want him around—she can't hear him when he walks into the room with her. It gives her the creeps."

"Okay. How about a burglar alarm system?"

"She says she'd have a heart attack if it went off in the middle of the night, so she'd be dead anyway."

"For God's sake! Get her a couple of big dogs."

"She's allergic to them."

We both laughed. I put the cup of tea on the floor next to the futon. "Has she called the police?"

"She did the first time, but they weren't very helpful. She won't call them again."

"Has she told Richard about all this?"

"No. She won't."

I took the next logical step. "She thinks he's behind it, doesn't she?"

"She hasn't said so, but yes, that's what she thinks."

"Then why does she stay in the house alone with him?"

"She says he's too much of a coward to do anything like that himself, or even have it done while he's around."

"Well, it doesn't make sense. He went after her when she went to Mexico, and he wants the marriage intact, if for no other reason than he's running for D.A."

"I know."

"So what has she done?"

"She's hired me."

"And you're supposed to find out who's after her."

"Yes. And I will."

"But who is after you, Lee?"

"I don't know."

"I thought you spotted him today."

"Not really." She looked toward the windows, her brows drawn together. "I had a peculiar feeling that whoever it was, was standing right across the street from us. When I got into the crowd, the feeling went away. So I walked for a while, just to see what would happen."

"I came after you, but I didn't see you. Where did you walk?"

She turned to me, ignoring the question. "You shouldn't have done that."

"Look, I don't want to make you queasy, but I don't like any of it. Someone's following you, I think someone's following me, and neither one of us seems to have any answers about anything."

Her eyes went to the windows again. The curtains were full but thin. Someone might be able to see through them with the light on in the room. I put my hand on her thigh. "Why do you keep looking at the windows?"

Her eyes moved back to me swiftly. "No reason," she said. Then, "Neal, are you frightened?"

As a matter of fact, I was. I could see the silver seal, his slick head tilted back so he could peer down at me even while he was sitting, the smugness on his face, the power behind the look. "I haven't been," I told her, "but I've got a bad feeling that it's stupid not to be."

We stared at each other a few moments, then I reached for the tea. The flowerlike smell of it made my nose twitch. I put it down again. "I could use a drink," I said.

"I figured you could." She got up and went across the room to her canvas bag. Out of it she pulled a fifth of Scotch. She held it up; it was about half full. She went to get a glass.

"Tell me what I did to deserve this," I said as she handed me the bottle and glass, "so I can do it again."

She curled her body beside me, and propped herself up on an elbow. "We all need our vices," she said.

"Yes," I conceded, "but what's yours?"

She smiled. "You."

•   •   •

As Lee and I fell into an exhausted sleep, the police, in cooperation with Chance Callahan's office, conducted the largest vice and narcotics raid to take place in New Orleans in years. It was like Washington crossing the Delaware on Christmas Day to surprise the Hessians: While the police were assumed to be occupied on the streets where the biggest party in the country was going on, they moved into the underworld and cleaned up.

19

Twice Violated

Lee told me the next morning that, when she was needed, her nights would belong to Paula Cotton. With Mardi Gras over, the Cottons' busy social life would be in a lull during Lent. My guess was that Paula would be spending a lot of time alone. Richard's campaign for district attorney along with his ongoing law practice would provide him with plenty of excuses to be away from home at night. Lee's plan was to be in the house with Paula or hidden outside until Paula's torturer was caught.

I offered to be the one hidden while she remained inside the house, but Lee said she would handle it solo. She didn't add what I already knew, that Paula Cotton had decided she disliked me intensely. Hysterical women make good-paying clients, but the fee is hard earned with placation.

St. Charles Avenue, at just after eight o'clock the morning after Mardi Gras, was close to being cleaned up, but it looked as if most of the litter had been moved into the lobby of the Euclid. The plants were strung with Mardi Gras beads.

My apartment, however, was neat as a pin, cleaner than it had been. Not even a stray glass was left to tell about the party; my mother wouldn't have slept well otherwise. But as I walked into the living room, I could hear a dripping sound, and it wasn't coming from the kitchen sink. I went from the sun-filled living room into the darkened bedroom. When I turned on the light, there was a loud streak of profanities. They came from my mouth.

The bedroom ceiling near the bathroom was sagging heavily, and water was steadily dripping from the center of the bulge; more was leaving shiny snail tracks on the wall between the bedroom and bathroom. The carpet was saturated, and water was splashing onto the bedspread. I pushed it back. The mattress and box springs were already wet, but nothing like they were going to be if the ceiling gave, and it looked as if it might go at any moment.

I went to the phone in the living room and called the manager's apartment. Anything past five rings was a waste of time; I hung up in the middle of the fifth. I would have tried the office downstairs, but I knew he never got there before nine, sometimes not before noon. The extra set of lock picks was in the drawer of the night table next to the bed. I took an apprehensive glance at the ceiling and dashed under it.

Waiting for the elevator would have been another waste of time. I took the stairs, three at once, and ran down the hallway to the apartment above mine. I pounded on the door, then immediately went to work on the lock.

If it'd been my apartment, I would've left it, too. The smell of rotting food was strong enough to move the furniture out. In the kitchen was a small delicatessen left to spoil; the living room deserved official designation as a new city dump. I kicked over a bucket of fried chicken trying to get through the apartment to the source of the trouble. The carpet at the far end of the living room squished under my feet.

It was clear that someone had cleverly seen the possibilities of the bathtub as an ice chest. Empty beer cans bobbed in the water or pirouetted slowly on the bottom of the tub. What was unclear was why a stream of water the size of a heart of palm had been left running. The drain near the top of the tub would have taken care of the overflow except that a label had soaked off a bottle of wine and blocked it. Water stood a quarter of an inch deep on the bathroom tiles, tipped over the threshold, and soaked through the carpet to run down the edge of the concrete flooring and find a low spot in my ceiling. I waded into the flood zone, turned off the water and unstopped the plug. Then I went to my apartment, took a shower, and put on a dark pin-striped suit fresh from the cleaners. I wrote a note to the manager, which I tacked to his door on the way downtown.

Leone's growl and the cup of coffee I got from her put life back into synch. I looked forward to reading the *Picayune* in my dry and comfortable office.

I didn't know about the raids yet. I took a copy of the paper off the stack on the counter of the newsstand across from the elevators, and there it was, plastered all over page one, bigger than Mardi Gras. The picture showed two portly handcuffed men trying to avert their faces from the camera. One was a judge on the criminal court; the other was a federal appeals court judge. I folded the paper and tucked it under my arm and headed for an open elevator.

But I wasn't going to get to read the paper right away. I unlocked the office door, and the first thing I saw through the open door of the waiting room was the mess of files strewn all over the floor of the inside room. It was a thorough, professional job. The file drawers and desk drawers had all been removed so that every possible nook could be scrutinized. Every sofa and chair cushion had been tested and tossed. The small rug was rolled up. In each corner the wall-to-wall carpet was pulled back. The shades were down. The light fixtures were in pieces, the sockets unscrewed from the walls. They wouldn't have missed a microchip. I threw the paper on the desk and scrambled through the files. Richard Cotton's file was gone.

I put the cushion back on the chair and sat at the desk. Very slowly, I straightened the desk, but my mind was working fast. I slammed the middle drawer back in place, and grabbed the phone.

His secretary answered.

"This is Neal Rafferty," I barked. "Put Callahan on."

The line froze between us. "Mr. Callahan is not taking any calls."

"He's taking this one. It's Rafferty." I spelled it.

She put me on hold. The next voice I heard was no surprise.
"This is Leonard Yastovich, Mr. Rafferty."

"I asked for Callahan."

"Mr. Callahan isn't taking calls this morning."

"I already heard that once."

"Well, if you read the morning newspaper, you know why."
There was a small laugh. I could see his puckered lips trying to let
loose. "It looks like you'll either have to talk to me or wait."

I swung my legs onto the desktop, leaning back in the chair.
"No, you'll do very nicely at that, Yastovich. Just ask your boss
this—ask him if he expected me to file it away all neat and
convenient for him under Richard Cotton's name." I waited. "Did
you get that, Yastovich?"

"I got it."

"And tell him not to bother with the apartment. It's not there
either." I hung up.

Three fingers drummed the desktop briefly, then my hand was
back on the phone. I called Richard Cotton's office. He wasn't in
yet. I left a message for him to call as soon as he got there. I
pushed the buttons and made one more phone call, to Mr. D.'s
Laundry, but there was no answer.

I reeled in the newspaper. Over eighty people had been busted
in simultaneous raids at a couple of barrooms, one in the French
Quarter, once across Basin Street where Storyville used to be, a
motel on Tulane Avenue, and, of all places, the Bucktown
Tavern. The two judges were rounded up at the motel where skin
flicks were being shown as a backdrop to live displays of various
forms of copulation, and cocaine was being passed around the
table. There were similar scenes taking place at the other
locations, along with bookmaking and a high-stakes poker game at
the Bucktown Tavern. Drugs, including cocaine, marijuana,
amphetamines and Quaaludes, were found at all of the locations.
The barrooms and the tavern were out of business—padlocked.
Clarence "Chance" Callahan's office was responsible for orches-
trating the raids, the result of months of investigation. Callahan
himself was quoted as saying that this was only "the tip of the

iceberg," that the vice operations were linked with organized crime, people "who have escaped our clutches before, but won't this time." He wouldn't release the details yet, that master of suspense. This would probably be worth weeks of free publicity to the silver seal.

There was another item worthy of interest. It was about the kid on the motorcycle who'd been gunned down by the cop. Callahan coolly explained that a half a million dollars' worth of cocaine and an unspecified amount of opium had been found in the kid's bedroom at his parents' home. This information had been withheld because the district attorney's office did not want to jeopardize their investigation. When he was asked specifically about the shooting, Callahan told the reporter that the black youth, although his record was clean, was a known drug dealer, and that he had been considered dangerous, possibly armed. In his opinion—and who else's counted?—no charges would be pressed against the policeman. He reminded the reporter of the youth's connection to the Bucktown Tavern, and, hence, to the bigger issue of organized crime. It always sounded good for the district attorney's office to be going up against the Mafia, but my guess was that after the election there would be no more talk about it.

As always, Callahan had an answer for everything. It was sweet, very sweet, and very glib. And Callahan's self-confidence was compelling.

But, I thought as I looked at the mess in my office, he wasn't confident about everything.

20

Runnin' Scared

A paying customer who walked in on me right now might decide to pay someone else, so I got busy straightening up, but not before I called Central Lockup to see if Mr. D. was there or had been sent down for arraignment. He had managed to escape the police net. One part of me was glad because I admired the street smarts of the boxy-faced sleazeball; the other part of me would have liked to see his back screwed to the wall so I could get a shot at making him talk.

It was going to take a few days to go through the files and put them back as they had been, but for now I put them in enough order that I could find something if I needed to. I tacked the carpet back down and went to work on the light fixtures. They were large and unwieldy. I had to move the desk out to the middle of the room to get to them. Then I had to move it back and get down on my hands and knees to find the missing screws in the tarnished metal–colored carpet. Half an hour on all fours and I began to feel hostile.

The afternoon dragged. The sun moved behind a tall building, and the office took on a twilight tone. Still nothing from Richard Cotton. I called his office again. His secretary told me he'd been in and left. She said she'd given him my message. I was about to call his house, reluctantly, when the phone rang. It was Lee.

"Don't come over," she said. "I'll be at the Cottons' tonight."

"Did Paula Cotton just call you?"

"Yes."

"Would she have called if Richard was there?"

"Probably not. Why?"

"I'm trying to track him down. She didn't say where he was, did she?"

"No, just that he said he'd be late."

I thought a moment. "Lee, do you have the Covington number?"

"Hold on." She was back in a few seconds and gave it to me. "Is something wrong?" she asked. "You sound agitated."

"Try aggravated. I'm wondering why Richard Cotton is making himself so scarce."

There was a pause, and I could tell we were each waiting for the other to say something informative. I spoke first. "I tell you what. If he isn't in Covington, I'll call you back, and when you get to his house, you can put one of the extensions outside, and we'll see if he answers that."

She laughed, and we joked around a bit about who might answer the phone, then she got serious again.

"Neal, when you talk to Richard Cotton, you aren't going to tell him I'm with his wife, are you?"

I mulled that over. "We're in a peculiar situation, aren't we?" She agreed. "Look," I told her, "I wouldn't break your confidence unless I had a damned good reason to. If I felt like I had to, I'd let you know first. I wish she'd tell him herself what's going on. Maybe *he'd* stay home with her."

"Maybe he wouldn't," she said.

"Yeah, maybe he wouldn't. Anyway, what I want to talk to him about has nothing to do with the problems between him and his wife." I heard her other line start buzzing. I said, "Call me when you get home."

She said she would.

I sat back and lit a cigarette. Just then I'd felt like telling Lee the whole thing. I didn't want it to seem as if we were working on opposite sides of the fence, because that was not the way it was at all. Not in my mind. I smoked for a while, wondering why the urge to lay it all out to her always hit me when it was impossible to do so, when there wasn't any time. Then I had this strange thought about the violence of the past affecting the future. A single act of violence—seeing it, or seeing the result of it—could train your reactions much more quickly than you could willfully train them yourself. It could produce fear or more violence. Or maybe alienation, isolation. I'd been thinking that I couldn't be really comfortable with anyone who didn't know about Myra and what had happened afterward. But maybe that was wrong. Maybe I didn't really feel comfortable with anyone who knew. Maurice was the only exception I could think of. Maybe I was sick and tired of it being part of me.

I wanted a drink, but decided to resist the temptation until I got home. Home, I thought with disgust, and immediately got a bottle and glass out of the supply cabinet. No telling what further acts of violation I would find when I got back to the Euclid. But there was certainly something I could do about it. I retrieved the bulk of the paper that I'd thrown in the wastebasket after tearing out the article about the raids, and turned to the classifieds—apartments for rent. I ran my finger down the "Above Canal" listing. I wanted something uptown, not too far from the office, and some privacy. I stopped at a one-bedroom that sounded good, but the address was in the low part of uptown that flooded regularly. I'd had enough water violation at the Euclid. And I wanted privacy, not isolation. I stopped looking at one-bedroom places. We'd need the extra room for the workout equipment. Here was one—"Private, two bedrooms, Garden District" . . . And then the phone rang.

"Rafferty? Danny Dideaux. You know—Mr. D."

"I know," I said. "I've got the tuxedo—"

"Forget the tux. Can you meet me tonight?"

"At the laundry?"

"Stay away from the laundry." He named a motel on Decatur Street and gave me the room number. "Six-thirty," he said. "And keep an eye on your back."

Since the Père Marquette garage closes at ten, I took the car out and parked it on the fringe of the central business district where the warehouses are. I went across Canal, up Chartres to a restaurant where I could get a quick meal. I ate, then I started walking in the opposite direction of the motel. It was six o'clock. I walked through Jackson Square, and got a cup of coffee at the Café du Monde. After that I took a stroll on the Moon Walk, which runs along the Mississippi. A tug pushed a barge upriver. Lights reflected on the water, making the river appear calm and peaceful instead of running with its deadly swirling currents. I stopped and smoked a cigarette. As far as I could tell I was as alone as Greta Garbo. I flipped the cigarette into the rocks below me, turned quickly and ran down the steps back onto Decatur Street. But I still didn't go to the motel. I crossed over to Royal Street, took Royal at a fast pace to Conti and ducked into the parking garage of the Royal Sonesta Hotel. I slipped into the pedestrian stairway in the garage, went halfway up and waited. I heard no footsteps behind me. I went on up, then through the garage and out on the Iberville side.

Even at the motel I took no chances. I passed Mr. D.'s floor, and waited outside the elevators. Five minutes later I called the elevator back up, sent it down three floors, then took the stairs down to Mr. D.'s room.

I knocked lightly. Mr. D. opened the door and pointed a gun at my belly.

He waved me in impatiently with the hardware. We nearly collided as he hurried to stick his cubic head out the door to look up and down the hallway. He locked the door and put the chain in its groove. His green alligator shoes slid across the carpet toward me. He stopped in front of the double dresser.

"I'm being watched," he said. The gun was still in his hand, but down, pointing at the floor.

"I didn't see anyone." I talked to the gun. "As far as I can tell, it's just you and me."

He followed my eyes, but held on to the piece. "You tell anyone you came to see me?" he demanded.

"No."

"No, but last week a blind man woulda known you were there," he said snidely.

"I didn't see any blind men," I said just as snidely.

"Then you wanna tell me why it is that ever since you paid me that little visit someone's been on my tail?"

"That night?" I asked, thinking that I hadn't picked up on anything until late the following afternoon.

He shrugged. "Yeah. You come over all hepped up about some film, the next thing I know, I gotta hind man."

"You spotted the tail that night—Thursday night?"

"Jesus, were you born yesterday, pal?" He shook his head with disgust. "When's the last time you spotted a good tail, huh, Rafferty? Look, I leave the laundry about half an hour after you. I come back early Friday 'cause I gotta big demand for the weekend, and the laundry's been hit." He pointed the gun at me. "You got any kinda idea the mess I was in? Film everywhere," he waved the gun around, "cans all over the place. I gotta save what I can, clean it, get the orders ready . . . the biggest weekend of the year—"

He was set to rave on, but I stepped forward and grabbed his wrist. "Do you mind?" I asked.

"Yeah. Awright." He put the gun on the dresser. His eyes snapped back to me. "You wanna hear this?" His voice went up about an octave.

"Sure," I said, "but I can concentrate better now."

"Jesus. Where was I? So I get everything together and go home. The next time I leave the place for longer than it takes to get a pack of smokes, the apartment gets hit. I go back there and it's like hurricane-ville, you know?"

"When was that?"

"Monday afternoon. I left it the way I found it and checked in here."

"Then the way I figure it, I picked up the tail from you. I was hit after that."

"When?"

"I don't know exactly. Sometime after three Monday, or early this morning. The building was locked up for Mardi Gras."

"Your office, huh? You been home yet?"

We looked at each other and mustered up a laugh between us. I pulled out a cigarette; he copped it from me. I pulled out another one and sat down on a piece of stick furniture.

"So you didn't go out all weekend?" I asked him.

"Uh-uh."

"No parades, no parties?"

"Uh-uh."

"Then you checked in here Monday afternoon."

"That's right."

"Did you go out yesterday?" He shook his head. "Interesting," I said.

"Whadaya mean?" Suspicious. A little hostile.

He was sitting on the foot of the bed. I put my elbows on my knees, leaning toward him. "I mean this, Danny: The laundry is broken into and you stay home all weekend. No parties, no fun. Your apartment is ransacked and you check into a motel. You're runnin' scared, Danny. You tell me."

He stood up and walked away from me, then he turned around and pointed with the two fingers that held the cigarette. "You said yourself the film got Marty killed."

"Yeah, but you don't have the film, and whoever searched your premises knows it's not at either place. What do you know about the film, Danny?"

He walked back to the ashtray he'd put on the bed, put out the cigarette, and walked back and forth in the space between the bed and the dresser.

When he stopped pacing, he came on strong. "What's your interest in this, Rafferty? Who's payin' you?"

"No one."

He jutted his chin at me. "Who was Marty blackmailing—you?"

"No."

"Then who?"

"I don't know that he was blackmailing anyone. I don't even know for sure there's a film."

He started hiking again, shaking his head, saying, "Uh-uh, uh-

uh." He wheeled around on the heel of an alligator loafer to face me. "I don' need this cop routine, pal. You're askin' a lotta questions, but you ain't comin' up wit' no answers." He sounded nasal and mean.

"I ain't checkin' into no motels, either, pal."

I tried to sound like I could get just as mean as he could, but I wasn't getting the desired results. Instead of getting nervous, Mr. D. relaxed. There was a smirk on his face. I had a feeling I was about to get an invitation to leave. I had to try something else.

"You're talking to an obsessed man, Danny." I lit a cigarette and tossed the pack and lighter on the bed. He stayed where he was. I sat back and took a long drag. "My interest in this was to prove to myself I was right, that Solarno murdered a girl five years ago."

"Well, you can't prove it by me, pal."

"I wasn't trying to. I was in Solarno's apartment after he was murdered. I found a piece of jewelry that belonged to her—a gold star."

He kept his eyes on me, and moved over to the bed to get a cigarette. "Wit' a diamond on it?" he asked. I nodded; he shook his head. "I know the piece you're talkin' about." He lit up, and talked around the cigarette. "Marty gave it to a stripper he pimped for. We were in the joint she worked at one night, and Marty ripped it off her neck because she didn't wanna turn a trick wit' some rich nigger."

"He ripped it off a dead girl first."

"Maybe, but I asked him afterward if he had to buy the girls diamonds to keep 'em in line. You know how Marty talked: He said it was a cheap bauble he let a friend pay 'im off wit' because he was short on cash."

"What did you expect him to say, that he'd taken it as a trophy after the kill?"

"He didn't have to say anything. He was pissed. His mind was on the nigger who'd already paid 'im for that particular girl."

"So?"

"Don't get mad at me, pal. I'm just passin' along what I was told."

I didn't say anything; I punched the cigarette out in the ashtray, getting ashes all over the bed.

Mr. D. picked up the ashtray and got the ashes off the bed. He put the ashtray on the dresser and sat on the edge of the piece of furniture, his ankles crossed and his arms folded. "So what's five years ago got to do wit' a film?" he asked.

"Not a damned thing. I'm telling you why I was in Solarno's apartment. While I was there I happened to notice that he had a projector all set up, but no films; the films were taken."

"Says you."

"Says the cops. They found a piece of one they assumed was ripped out of the projector."

One slime-green shoe tapped up against the other one, but the reptile look was in his eyes. "Who're you workin' for, Rafferty— Callahan?"

"No," I said slowly, "but you're asking the right questions now."

21

Pal Danny

Mr. D. wasn't satisfied until I told him a cop friend had let me into Solarno's apartment, and I explained to him that I'd only become interested in this film business after Callahan threatened me. I implied that I'd gone to see Callahan initially about the five-year-old murder, but that after I mentioned the film I was followed. The office was broken into, and if someone was afraid I knew about something, then there must be something to know.

Mr. D. scrutinized me closely while I talked. When I finished he pushed himself off the dresser, rattling the drawers. "Sounds pretty good," he commented.

"Sounds a whole lot better than anything you've told me yet," I said testily.

He sat on the foot of the bed, and fooled around lighting a cigarette, sizing me up out of the corner of his eye. He spit out some smoke and then he started. "Marty came over to the laundry a coupla days before they got 'im. He was all jacked up over some investigative work he was doin'. He said he was gonna get himself back in the good graces of the fag." He stopped.

"Callahan," I said.

He nodded. "Marty was Callahan's bagman. He liked bein' on the D.A.'s staff—it made him feel important. He was pissed that Callahan got rid of him. Callahan isn't clean, you understand, it's just that Marty's mouth was too big. And he was too unreliable. I figured Marty'd found a way to put the squeeze on Callahan so he could get back on the staff. When he turned up dead, I figured Callahan had decided to get rid of him once and for all."

He got up, walked around, and put out the cigarette. "Then you show up talkin' about this film Marty wanted to show. Right then I figure there's someone else in the picture." He waited, but I had no comment. "Marty never said nothin' to me about no film."

"If there was a film, do you think he would've?" I asked.

"Hard to say. For all I know, he was makin' up stories again. He coulda been tellin' Callahan one thing, somebody else another. Marty was best at playin' two people that way, and soakin' 'em both."

"So you're saying maybe there is no film."

"I'm sayin' I don't know," he said impatiently. "I figure you can get a line on that from someone else."

"Well, you're wrong." I got up and walked past him and leaned against the wall on the other side of the room. He watched me, ready for a fast one. "You picked a convenient time to hole up, Danny—it got you off the street just in time for Tuesday night's roundup."

"Do you have any idea what that cost me, Rafferty? Almost every film I had left was confiscated in those raids."

"I'd say that's a small price. It could've been a lot worse."

"You sayin' I knew about the raids? Then why am I still here, smart man?"

"That's the part that's bothering me. You're too scared, and I don't get it. Unless you're blackmailing Callahan."

"You got quite an imagination, pal."

"That I do. I can imagine that any number of people might have wanted to kill Solarno. I can imagine that Callahan might have been one of them. I can also imagine that you might've been in on the deal with Solarno, except that you didn't scare until over a week after he was dead. Something's missing here, and it smells like blackmail to me. You said yourself that Callahan isn't clean. Maybe what you know buys you some information, like when the raids are going to happen. Maybe you're afraid that what you know will buy you a death like Solarno's."

That made him sweat. The thought of getting sliced like that would make anyone sweat. He went over to the window, pushed the drape back with a finger and peeked out. He came back to the middle of the room wiping the space above his upper lip.

He struck his chest with his fist. "You wanna know why I'm scared, man? Because it doesn't add up"—he swept the air in front of him with the flat of his hand—"nothin' adds up. I been in this business since I was sixteen years old. I've done my share of payin' off, and I've gotten my share, too. That's the way it goes: One hand pays off the cops, the other one gets it back somewhere else. But this time it's different. Yeah, I knew about the raids. And I paid for the information—get the films out to the places, and let 'em know where they went. So why am I bein' watched? Why am I bein' searched? I did my part, and all of a sudden nobody's talkin' to me."

"You mean Callahan?"

"No. My informant."

"Someone in the D.A.'s office?"

"No comment."

That got me irritated. I moved off the wall toward him. "Wise up, Mr. D. How do you expect to find out anything while you're sitting in a motel room? Who's not talking to you?" I gave him a minute, then I said, "It's a good shot that whoever's watching you is watching me, too, but I'm not planning to sit around and do nothing about it."

"Awright. A guy named Yastovich," he said. "But so help me, Rafferty, you spill it . . ."

"Save it." I laughed. "Good ol' Yastovich. When's the last time you talked to him?"

"Thursday. I tried to get him Friday, again on Monday. On Monday, get this, a secretary tells me to hold on, then she gets back on the phone and asks me if the films are out to the places. She asks me if there's some problem. I tell her yeah, there's a problem. She says, but the films are out to the places. I told her the goddamn films were where I said they would be. She says Yastovich will be in touch. I called all day today. All of a sudden he ain't takin' my calls."

Mr. D. was sweating freely now. He pulled his shirttails out of his pants and unbuttoned his shirt two more buttons. His chest was hairless, his shoulders big and bony looking under the polyester shirt. He sat down in the chair I'd vacated.

"So you think Yastovich, or Callahan, is having you watched, searching your places."

"It's where I'd put my money, pal."

"Why? You cooperated. There has to be a reason. Did you tell Yastovich something you know about Callahan? You think Yastovich squealed?"

He jumped out of the chair. "What do you think I know, Rafferty? What do you think I know that if I put the squeeze on Callahan I wouldn't end up as dead as Solarno?" He was trying hard to keep his voice down.

"I don't know. That's what I'm trying to figure out."

And I thought about it, letting Mr. D. wear the carpet thin while I smoked a cigarette and he calmed down.

I backtracked to what seemed like some kind of starting point. "You said you let them know where the films were; you told the secretary that the films were where you said they would be. How did the places get picked? *You* picked them?"

He gave me a look full of hatred. "I don't need to talk to you, Rafferty. Why don't you buzz off." I guess he'd decided he didn't like me anymore because he'd lost his cool in front of me.

"You called *me*, Danny." I talked to him quietly. "You said you were scared. You want to get to the bottom of this?" I took silence as an affirmative and went on. "What about the places the films went to?"

"It wasn't the places, it was the people," he said grudgingly. I asked him if he'd like to elaborate. "Like the judges," he said, "they always used a motel. I had to let them know where."

"Who was it at the Bucktown Tavern?"

"I don't know. That was different. Yastovich told me to bring the films there."

"That was the first time you ever went there?"

"No. They used to close the place up for private parties. They closed for Mardi Gras day."

"So the other people came to you, but not the Bucktown Tavern people?" He nodded. "Who owns the tavern? The mob?" He shrugged. "And that kid on the motorcycle, the busboy from the tavern who was gunned down by the cop—you believe he ran dope for the mob?"

"I believe he ran dope for somebody."

"For Callahan," I said, and I could feel my adrenaline kick in. Something was coming together here. I didn't quite have a grip on it, but I was close. Mr. D. wasn't agreeing or disagreeing, but he'd given up his grudge for a nasty smile. He reached for a cigarette.

I stood there trying to grab on to something that was going to make it all click right into place. Only it wasn't happening. Maybe it wasn't going to happen. The adrenaline kick calmed down. I thought about Richard. He went to the Bucktown Tavern to drink beer with the residents of Bucktown who were his clients. Did one of his clients own the tavern? I doubted it. They'd gotten a lot of publicity since the flooding had started in New Orleans. As far as I knew they were all struggling fishermen who needed to stay on their rent-free land. That made me think of the fishermen unloading the crabs that night I went to see Richard at the tavern, and that's when it clicked.

Those nice round-bottomed Lafitte skiffs. I could picture them dragging their nets out in the Gulf of Mexico, a romantic picture against the backdrop of a red sunset I'd seen a thousand times, prints in artists' studios in the French Quarter, captured on pieces of slate, paintings hanging on the fence around Jackson Square. Now I could see that Lafitte skiff chugging its way to a meeting place on a certain latitude out in the Gulf, chugging its way back to the dock behind the tavern, cocaine unloaded in seafood crates.

"The tavern was where the drugs came in," I said to Mr. D. "And the kid—he was running dope out of the tavern for Callahan, except he was stealing part of it, bringing it home, stashing it."

"Bing-o," said Mr. D.

"That's what Solarno found out." I was excited now. "Yastovich made sure you got films to the tavern and that there was plenty of coke going around so the tavern could be raided and shut down."

"And that's the problem, pal—there ain't no more tavern. Just like there ain't no more Solarno."

"No, but there's Yastovich."

There was also one thing that was still bothering me, that I had no explanation for. "Ever hear of a Christopher Raven?"

"Sure," he said, and smiled that nasty smile. "I heard he was found burned up in some posh uptown fireplace."

He was getting on my nerves. "Did you know him?" I snapped.

His bony shoulders came up close to his ears. "I'd seen him around." He could see I was ready to turn nasty now, so he added, still smiling, "At the Bucktown Tavern. He was a busboy, too."

I thought about it for a few seconds, and then I decided to go with it. "Does a man named Richard Cotton ever come to the laundry?"

He gave a low nasal laugh. "Not anymore." His sharp-edged smile cut deeper into his face. "He sends his nigger."

22

The Alleyway

After telling Mr. D. to stay put until I got back to him, I left
the motel and crossed Canal with a third eyeball attached to my
spine. The big city noises receded as I walked deeper into the quiet
of the dark warehouse district, movements of cars and people
muffled by the heavy humidity and the thick brick walls of the
buildings until they became a steady hum indistinguishable from
my own brain waves. In the dense silence my heels hit the
concrete like a pile driver making its way down the street. I
thought it might be time to follow the ranks of joggers as far as the
shoe store.

I stopped to light a cigarette, then the spongy darkness closed in
around me again. The area was eerie at night, deserted at the end
of the workday, the rusted doors closed and immovable looking,
an iron and brick ghost town.

The warehouses were a slim sidewalk away from the street.
Between some of them there were spaces wide enough for big
trucks to back up to loading ramps; others were separated by
alleyways narrowed by dumpsters and piles of corrugated boxes and
other rubble. My car was parked about three blocks down a little
ahead of just such a narrow alleyway. I started walking more
quickly toward it, my presence on the street alien and inappro-
priate.

As I got deeper into the gloom, I began to feel spooked. I didn't think I'd been followed, but the sense of another presence was very strong. I slowed my pace for a few steps, then stopped walking altogether. The hum of traffic seemed loud now—it was all I could hear. I flicked the cigarette into the street and turned around. In the wet air Canal Street was a haze of light at the end of a tunnel. From it the isolated honking of a horn penetrated the hum. After that the silence was denser, more complete. A few seconds passed. Off in the distance a police siren began to wail. I waited for it to get closer, but it died away. I turned again and headed for the car, less than half a block from me. My body was tensed; my right hand was foolishly empty. It reached into my pocket and got out the car keys.

They made their move as I bent to put the key in the lock. They jumped from the alleyway, and even with my back turned I knew it was two of them. My right elbow sprung back and dug under the rib cage of one of them. I heard a short grunt and caught a glimpse of a face with a pair of glasses on it as my arm came back around, my body twisting to throw its weight into the swing. I was sapped behind the left ear before I could finish the pivot.

My legs gave way and somebody grabbed me under the arms, dragging me backward as I fought to stay conscious. I tried to move my legs, to get some traction, but I couldn't. Then I thought pushing might be easier, so I tried to push off with my heels, to shove into the person behind me, but although my brain gave the command, my body didn't obey. The next thing, I was falling, falling. It seemed as if I fell a long way before my back thudded on the concrete. I was vaguely aware of my shoulder striking something sharp. I was also aware that I'd been dragged into the alleyway, but I wanted to see that face again, and the face of the other one. Then my head bounced. I must have blacked out because I didn't remember my hands being secured or the enormous pressure on my chest. There was also something in my left eye, at the outside corner. I tried to flutter my eyelids to get rid of it, but it only stuck deeper, causing me to cry out.

"Don't open your eye or I'll cut it," someone said in a harsh, low, gravelly voice that was almost a whisper.

He spoke from above me, from on top of my chest. His breath was warm on my face; it smelled like refried beans.

"Tell me why I shouldn't kill you," he said, and the rocks in his voice gurgled against one another.

You shouldn't kill me because I don't want to die, I thought, but I didn't say it out loud because before I could he increased the pressure on the knife, cutting my eye, then slowly dragging the knife down, down to the bone, down toward my ear. I heard the sound an animal makes when it knows it's going to die, and I knew it came from me because there was no one else there who could have made that sound.

They say that before you die your whole life flashes before you in a few seconds. I have never believed that, and indeed it isn't true. What flashed in front of me were the details of Marty Solarno's death. I saw him tied down, the two men with him, one hovering just above his face, and Solarno making the sound I'd just made over and over again, and I heard Uncle Roddy talking to the pathologist about what I'd had for dinner. Then one of the men with Solarno, the only one whose face I could see, went over to the corner of the room and puked. I knew that face, the face wearing the glasses.

"No, no!" he hissed behind me. "Warn him!" It was urgent; maybe he was going to throw up again.

The rocks in the voice gurgled, laughter, and the slice was finished. I was as out of breath as I would have been after running a mile, but I couldn't catch my breath because he was sitting on me. I tried to pay no attention to the blood filling my ear.

If I was going to die, I was going to say the name of the one I knew. I wanted him to hear me say it forever. And I was going to open my eyes. The pain in the left eye was bad enough to keep either eye from snapping open. As I tried to open them, I heard a third voice. It was pitched high, shrill. It wasn't in the alleyway.

"Police! Freeze!"

The man nearly crushed my chest getting off it. My eyes opened in time to see his shoe coming for my face. I flinched, and he caught me on the corner of my chin. Behind me, cardboard boxes fell, and there was a lot of scuffling as people fled down the alleyway. The next sound I heard was a "whumpf," not loud, and by the time I was able to get up and look in the direction I'd heard everyone going, there was nothing. No one.

I took a couple of steps to the mouth of the alley, and looked up and down the street. No police unit waited for the officer who had given chase to my assailants. I turned in the other direction, to go through the alley, my shoulder rising to my jawline periodically to keep some of the blood from running down my neck.

My hands were bound together with one of those plastic tie wraps that are used to hold large clumps of wires together by electricians and phone company workers, and also by the police when there are more people who need to be arrested than there are handcuffs. I used my two hands together as a club to move boxes aside, and that's when I saw him, and when I knew what the soft "whumpf" I'd heard was. He was lying just beyond the boxes, face down, with a knife sticking out of his back. I put my hands under his cheek and lifted his head to see his face better in the dark. His glasses had been knocked askew when he fell; one of the lenses was cracked. I let his cheek rest again on the cold concrete, and felt for the pulse in his neck just to make sure.

"Damn," I said.

I couldn't question a dead man, and Leonard Yastovich was very dead.

23

Not Even a Body

In the dark with one eye shut it was difficult to find anything to cut through the plastic tie wrap. I had already tried to snap it by pushing the heels of my hands together and exerting pressure on it, but it was too strong. I looked for the sharp object I'd fallen on, but I couldn't find it, unless it was the corner of a heavy corrugated box. I ended by standing at the right angle that joined the front and side of one of the buildings and sawing through the tie wrap with the edge of a rough brick. By that time it felt like most of the blood had drained out of my body through my eye and face, and the outside edges of my hands and wrists were bloody from scraping on the bricks.

I put the tie wrap in my pants pocket, and took off my jacket, turning the lining out to press it up against my cheekbone. All around the slash and in my eye it felt as though tiny jackhammers were chipping away at flesh and bone and eyeball. I went for the car keys, and remembered I'd had them out when I'd been attacked. I bent down to search for them and the jackhammers grew larger, the side of my face heavy with the pounding of them.

A few decades went by before I found the keys in the gutter, almost under the rear wheel of the car. I stood up to fumble at the lock, my head woozy, my legs almost as weak as they'd been when I got sapped.

It was when I started driving and tried to open my eye that I began to be afraid I'd lost it. The eye didn't want to open, or maybe it was sealed shut. I decided it was better not to know if I could see anything out of it, so I left it alone, but every movement of the good eye caused a lot of pain in the closed one. The aggravation was so great that by the time I drove the few blocks to the Père Marquette, I was more angry that I might lose the sight in it than afraid.

I parked in a freight zone in front of the building and stumbled into the lobby. Before anything could come out of the open mouth of the security guard, I shot a number at him and told him to get Lieutenant Rankin on the phone. One of the walls held me up while he did it.

Uncle Roddy had enough details to get him over to the warehouse district in a hurry, and I went up to the office. The first thing I did was throw my jacket in the trash can and take a long snort from the bottle that was still sitting on my desk. Then I went over to the sink that was hanging on the wall behind a folding screen in the corner of the room and stood in front of the mirror above it. Very gently, I pried my eyelid open. The eye gushed like a geyser, but at least I was getting a blurred image through the water. I let it close again, and washed up. The cut was still oozing. It went in an arc from the eyelid almost to the tip of my ear, like the marking on a tabby. The cutter was apparently into symmetry, so I suppose I should feel lucky not to have a matching stripe on the other side. But what I felt was another surge of rage which pumped enough adrenaline into me to get a wad of bandaging taped to the slice and me into my car.

Lights from three police cars careened and bounced off the fronts of the warehouses off Canal. One of the cars was horizontal in the street so its headlights could shine into the alley. An empty stretcher was on the sidewalk next to a crash truck.

I pulled up to the curb on the opposite side of the street. Uncle Roddy limped slowly toward me. He looked tired and irritated. I got out of the car and stood beside the open door, leaning against it. Uncle Roddy's eyes left my bandaged face and took in my shirt, one side of which was bloodsoaked to the waistline. His irritation seeped away, but his first question threw me.

"This the right alley?"

"Yes."

"There's no body in it."

I made a move to cross the street. One of his thick arms came up and blocked me.

"It's not there," he repeated.

Fonte came out of the hubbub in the alley. He was halfway to us when Uncle Roddy caught him in his peripheral vision. He didn't turn around, but waggled a hand in Fonte's direction. Fonte retreated.

"What went on here, Neal?"

I gave him the answer to his question, offering no further information except to say, "Whoever it was did the design on Solarno's face."

"Why you?" he wanted to know.

"The word on the street is that Solarno was trying to force his way back on Callahan's staff," I told him, "and Callahan thinks I know whatever it is Solarno had on him. After Solarno was murdered, I tried to talk to Callahan. First he threatened me, then he told me he was doing me a favor to tell me to lay off the Solarno business. I didn't know if Solarno really had anything, but I didn't deny knowing he did, either. When I got to the office this morning, it was in pieces. They even looked under the carpet and in the light fixtures. So I have to assume that Callahan believes or Solarno told him there was something tangible. I called his office, but he wouldn't talk to me. I talked to Leonard Yastovich instead, told him not to bother with my apartment, what he's looking for isn't there either."

Uncle Roddy put his hand over his eyes and forehead and rubbed hard. "Jesus!" he said. When the hand came down, the irritation was back, worse. "Don't you *learn*, Neal?"

"What? To lay off the politicos? Don't you hear what you're saying? If Callahan had Solarno murdered, why should he get away with it?"

"So all of a sudden you give a fuck who murdered Marty Solarno?" He was furious now. He came close to my face. "The man who murdered Myra Ledet?"

The side of my face felt like it was splitting open. Our noses were about three inches away from each other's. "I give a fuck who's trying to murder *me*!" I backed away and leaned on the car. "Let's stop this," I said. "I'm trying to say that if Callahan gets away with this, he'll think he can get away with anything."

He was in no way calmed down. "You say exactly what you wanna say. What you don't say is why you *really* wanted into Solarno's apartment, or what your motives are for diggin' around in Solarno's death, or why you wanted to talk to Callahan, why you didn't deny any knowledge of blackmail evidence, how you get your information about the word on the street, not even where you went tonight that you would park your car in a deserted part of town. And I know exactly what I would get if I asked any of those questions. Nothin'! I don't even get a body!"

"Look, Uncle Roddy, I didn't know what Solarno was after when I went to see Callahan, but I know now. Solarno knew Callahan was connected with a drug operation running out of the Bucktown Tavern. He'd figured out that the tavern was where the drugs were coming in from South America. What I don't know is if he managed to tie Callahan directly to the tavern or not. I was on my way to Yastovich when this happened."

"That doesn't even answer half my questions."

"There's a guy in a motel in the French Quarter who has some of the answers, Uncle Roddy."

"Let's go get him."

"Let me bring him to you."

"Oh, Mr. Big," he yelled, "runnin' the goddamn police department!"

I knew he could have raved on but I put a hand on his arm. "He's scared, Uncle Roddy. Callahan has used him. Now he thinks Callahan is trying to kill him. If a bunch of police show up to get him, he may never talk again."

He was sweating even though the night air was cool enough

that I was beginning to feel cold. "Go get your face sewn up," he said in a more normal tone of voice. "Come see me when everybody's ready to talk." He turned and shuffled away, his big back rounded with the effort of dragging his leg. He got to the middle of the street and stopped. He showed his profile and said, "Make it soon, Neal. Your guardian angel might not always know where to find you."

24

Because of Myra

The closest emergency room was at Charity Hospital, downtown on Tulane Avenue. The doctor who worked on me said my eyelid had been penetrated and the cornea badly scratched, but the eye itself was all right. I told him I was surprised that a scratched cornea could hurt that bad. He smiled but made no comment and asked no questions. Most of the victims of street violence end up at Charity, and he'd probably lost his curiosity after the first few days on the job. He put my eyelid back together and worked his way down my face. I lost count of the sutures somewhere in the twenties.

It was just before midnight when I got back to the Euclid. I was going to clean up, then go to the motel to get Mr. D.

The side of my face was numb, but the scratched cornea made up for that. I knew, though, that when the local anesthetic wore off I was in for some pain. I put a lot of ice in a dish towel and left it in the freezer, ready for when I needed it. The only liquor left in the house after Mardi Gras was bourbon. I took the bottle into the bedroom with me.

I had completely forgotten about all the water, but the biggest shock was that it had been taken care of. There was a hole in the ceiling where it had been drained, and the carpet had been removed. Along with a few pieces of plaster on the bedspread, there was a note from the manager that the ceiling would be replastered and a new carpet put in the next day. It was the quickest action I'd ever gotten at the Euclid.

My bloodstained shirt got pitched. I was heading to the shower when the temptation to lie down overcame the desire to get clean. I pulled back the bedding so I could lie down and close my good eye to keep it from irritating the other one. They'd put a patch on it and told me to keep it covered until I saw an eye specialist. I lay down with the bottle of bourbon cradled in my arm and thought about checking with the answering service to see if Richard Cotton had called . . . and thought that the workers being in the apartment had probably kept it from being rifled . . . wondering who had saved me . . . wondering if Lee was home . . .

I bolted into an upright position, nearly upsetting the bourbon, my heartbeat in my jawline. Whoever had waited for me at my car could have followed me to Lee's at another time, and if he'd tried me and Mr. D., he could decide to try Lee, and if he had slashed my face . . .

I scrambled off the bed, grabbed the phone, and called Lee's apartment. I let it ring and ring while I dragged it over to the drawer where I kept my gun. It kept ringing while I spun the chamber and loaded it. I slammed the receiver down and pulled out a shirt. While I was fumbling with buttons, there was a knock at the door. I knew it wasn't Uncle Roddy because it wasn't a bossy knock, and I have to admit I wouldn't have minded seeing him or even Phil Fonte just then. I made sure there was a bullet under the hammer, pulled the hammer back, and went to the door. There was another knock as I approached.

I put my hand on the doorknob, turned it and flung the door open. I pointed the gun right at Lee's heart.

The movement was so fast that I felt it almost before I saw it as she karate-chopped the gun from my hand. It hit the doorframe and bounced into the outside hallway without going off.

"Good God!" I exclaimed, wondering if I should take the cure.

"Sorry," Lee said. "Reflex." She picked up the gun, released the hammer and handed it to me.

I pulled her to me, and held her, waiting for my heart to quiet down some.

She moved back to look at my face. "Is your eye going to be okay?" she asked.

"Yes."

"That's good." She hid her face in my neck for a minute. I smiled at the empty doorway—she was worried.

She closed the door and went into the living room.

I followed her. "Did anything happen at the Cottons'?"

"No."

"Is Cotton at home?"

"He wasn't when I left, but she's expecting him." She held up a hand. "I have to call the answering service."

She told them to phone her immediately at my number if she got any calls. As she talked she turned to look at me. Still somewhat stunned, I looked back, at her eyes first, then her mouth, which smiled at me, her upper lip coming up over her crooked teeth, curving down to meet her lower lip. My heart squeezed in an extra pump, and my one eye traveled, taking in her efficient and deceptively strong body. She had on those tight black jeans she'd been wearing the first time I saw her. Into them was tucked a black turtleneck, its sleeves pushed almost to her elbows. She wasn't wearing a belt. On her feet were gold Nike running shoes with tan suede trim. She was slim, girlish, healthy and sexy. You wouldn't think she pumped iron or could neatly karate-chop a gun out of some unsuspecting sap's hand. I wondered what else she could do with such ease and nonchalance without getting overheated or breathing hard or getting in the least bit ruffled. I suddenly felt tired and old, out of shape and too damned vulnerable. I was going to have to stop and take stock of myself. Tomorrow.

I went into the bedroom, put the gun on the bedside table and located the bottle of bourbon. The shock had unfrozen the side of my face and it was beginning to ache. I sat on the foot of the bed.

Lee came in and sat down beside me. She looked at the floor, shuffling her foot on the exposed concrete. I pointed at the ceiling and told her about the bathtub overflowing upstairs.

"The thing about today," I said wearily, "is that even if I'd known I should, I couldn't have stayed in bed all day." I was staring morosely at the bottle in my hands.

"Well, at least your sense of humor is still intact." She nudged me.

She was sitting on my left side, so I had to turn my body to give her an evil eye. She reached up and fingered my blood-matted hair.

She took the bourbon away from me and put it on the dresser. "Come on," she said, tugging at my arm.

"What. I'm in pain."

"I'm going to clean you up—you'll feel better. Get undressed." She went into the bathroom and started drawing a bath.

I stood up and was fumbling with shirt buttons again. She pushed my hands away and sort of snapped me out of my clothes.

"Don't you even want to know what happened to me?" I was acting put out, but I wasn't.

"Every detail," she said, "after I give you a bath and get you comfortable."

I let her take over. It was tough getting the blood out of my hair without getting the bandages wet, but she managed.

"It's a good thing you came over," I said.

"It certainly is."

I opened the good eye and looked out of the side of it at her. My head was tilted back so she could rinse my hair. "It's a good thing I didn't shoot you."

She glanced down at me. "Not a chance." She soaped up a washcloth.

"Hm. Don't you know you're not supposed to hit someone who's holding a gun on you?"

"No."

"What are you—some kind of karate expert?"

"I'm rusty."

I tried to lift my eyebrows. My eyes involuntarily rolled, and I ended up squinting. She started soaping my back.

"Your shoulder's all scraped up," she said.

"That happened when I fell."

She lifted my arm that was furthest from her and turned it over. "You're all scraped up here, too," she informed me. She looked at the other one.

"That happened on the side of a brick building." She shook her head at me. I smiled. "Do you think men with scars on their faces are sexy?"

Her lip did its thing. "Some men are sexy with patches and bandages on their faces."

She put me in bed with the bourbon and the ice pack, and was changing into her blue-flowered kimono. I started to tell her I had to go back downtown, but then I decided that Mr. D. was safe for the night and that I was feeling too weak to move. It was too late, anyway. I should have let Uncle Roddy go get him.

I settled down into the covers, took a long, slow slug from the bottle and concentrated on watching Lee change instead of on the fact that I had a face with a three-inch gash in it.

"Did you feel at all like you were being followed today?" I asked her.

"No. I didn't worry about it too much on the way to the office this morning, but I drove around before I went to the Cottons'. Then I parked around the corner and walked."

"Did you go home first?"

"No. I had everything I needed downtown."

I told her about the office being broken into, and that I was afraid when she went home she would find her place in a shambles.

"I don't think so," she said, getting in bed beside me. "I've had the feeling that whoever followed me wasn't threatening me. I'm not saying I'm exactly relaxed, though." She sat up to face me and crossed her legs lotus fashion. "You know, Neal, the things we're working on aren't necessarily related."

I halted the bottle on its way to my mouth. "I get the feeling that you'd prefer they not be."

She rocked her body forward slightly. "I'm just not making any assumptions."

"Well, I'm not ruling it out."

She rocked back. "No. Of course not."

I swilled the bourbon. "Don't panic," I told her, "I'm training myself not to worry about you. After tonight, there shouldn't be a problem."

She hit me lightly on the leg. "Give me something to make some assumptions with."

We had managed to back off from an area of tension I didn't think we were capable of talking out yet. I hated thinking there was any kind of competitive feeling between us. I hated even more that I might be thinking there was one because of the old man's unwanted influence over me. I decided I was too fog-brained to deal with anything other than facts.

I started telling her about everything, beginning with the showdown with Callahan in his office, then the phone call to Yastovich after the break-in at my office, the meeting with Mr. D., the attack on me, the strange way I'd been saved and the disappearance of Yastovich's body. I ended by remarking that Richard Cotton was being elusive. I was drinking steadily the whole time I talked. The pain in my face had been reduced to a dull throb.

Lee sat in her lotus position, meditative. My eye wanted to close. I was barely managing to hold it at half-mast. I scrunched down and moved the pillows so they were supporting the ice pack.

"For a detective without a case," Lee said, "you've been seeing a lot of action."

"Um." My eyelids met. They couldn't help it—they wanted to be together.

Lee shook my leg. "Neal." The lids parted reluctantly. I squinted at her. "So you got into this battle with Callahan because of Richard Cotton?"

"More or less."

"The favor he asked you to do—he asked you to find out what Solarno had on Callahan?"

"Yeah." It was getting difficult to talk.

"But how did he know Solarno had anything?"

I couldn't keep squinting. I let the eyelid fall. "He hired Solarno to get something," I said sleepily.

She made a soft exclamation. "He wanted to win that badly? Why did you agree to help him?"

It had all gone too far for me to be sure anymore, but behind my closed eyelids appeared a vision of Myra. Because of Myra, I wanted to say, but she wouldn't understand that, and I couldn't go into it now. And, anyway, I was asking myself, why had I gone on with it after I'd found out it was Solarno who'd killed Myra? Why hadn't I told Richard I wanted out then? Wasn't I satisfied with that answer? I was suddenly very confused, but too tired to make much of the confusion.

Lee was saying something about the police, then, "I wouldn't have touched it."

I think I told her I knew she wouldn't have, but I'd had to, though I may have fallen asleep before I said that. Whether I said it or thought it, there seemed to be an end to the confusion just before I drifted off. It was simply that I'd had to do it.

The next thing I knew, the phone was ringing. I opened my eye expecting to see daylight, but it was dark. Lee was stirring beside me. I turned to reach the phone. The pillow was cold and wet. I shoved the dish towel and what was left of the ice on the floor, and picked up the receiver. It was Lee's answering service. I handed her the phone.

She listened, then I could hear the little beeps as she called a number. I moved the phone cord off my neck. I was going out again.

Lee reached over me to hang up the phone.

"It was Paula Cotton," she said. "Her husband hasn't come home."

"What time is it?" I muttered.

"It's two-thirty. I'll call you in the morning."

I didn't hear her go.

25

Hurricane-ville

The plasterer got me out of bed the next morning. I was slightly hung over, which slowed up the jackhammers.

Before I left the apartment I made a few calls. There were no messages at my answering service. Lee's service answered at her office; there was no answer at her apartment. Richard was not at his office. He wasn't at home either; no one was. I didn't know whether to be irritated or worried. Then I called the motel. Mr. D. wasn't in his room. The not-quite headache became full blown. I took a couple of aspirin and headed downtown.

Mr. D.'s room at the Decatur Street motel was completely cleaned out and cleaned up when I got there. The clerk downstairs smelled private cop all over me, and I had to part with twenty bucks to get into the room and find out that Mr. D. had not checked out. For another twenty, he got the night clerk on the phone, who told me sleepily that he didn't know what Mr. D. looked like so he didn't know if he'd seen him leave or not. I gave him a description. He said he didn't remember anyone like that. My guess was that Mr. D. had skipped out on the motel bill. Trying not to lose the faith, though, I left a message marked urgent for him. The only thing else my money bought me was what Mr. D. had put down as his home address—the laundry.

The next logical move was to run over to the laundry and peer into its dark, abandoned recess. I spent the rest of the afternoon going in and out of the establishments on Bourbon Street, trying to pry open countless pairs of tight lips and get a line on where Mr. D. lived. A woman in a joint called Daddy-O's finally believed it was a matter of life or death. Or maybe it was my bandaged face.

I spent time going in and out of the barrooms and strip joints instead of going to the city directory for Mr. D.'s address because I wanted the word out on the street that I was looking for him.

His apartment was two back rooms in a dumpy old house in the Faubourg Marigny, across Esplanade from the French Quarter. If he'd gone home, it hadn't been for long; his place was still a wreck—hurricane-ville, you know.

I used a credit card on the door and stepped into a rubble of cut-up clothes and yards of twisted celluloid. The whole place stank. In the kitchen the contents of the refrigerator had been dumped on the floor. In the bedroom was another lingering smell: The mattress had been slashed, wads of stuffing pulled out of it and urinated on. My office had only been searched; Mr. D.'s apartment was a message of hate and destruction. On the bathroom wall it was spelled out in big red letters: YOU DIE SCUM.

Hurricane-ville. Right.

I put an index finger on one of the letters and rubbed the stuff with my thumb. It was greasy, lightly fragrant. Lipstick. In the medicine cabinet I found a round plastic container of pancake makeup and a box of rouge. No lipstick.

When I'd told Mr. D. that I wasn't the one checking into motels, I don't know why he didn't slug me. Nothing made any sense but fear.

I needed to think; I needed to find a man I could only identify by voice. I needed to find someone else who was possibly the only person to see his face, my guardian angel. Mr. D. might know the identity of the raspy-voiced knife artist, but all I could do was wait for him to call me, probably from another motel. After seeing his apartment, I could understand that Mr. D. would consider my knowing where he was a risk. Besides Mr. D., there was Callahan. I might be able to get to the silver seal with a small army or a tank.

I had neither. Uncle Roddy, of course, was a small tank, but I had no ammunition to give him.

Two blocks before I got to the Père Marquette I was overcome by a compulsion to go across the lake. I took a left and went to the expressway entrance on Loyola Avenue.

The afternoon was overcast, hazy, and the air was muggy. It was unseasonably warm for March. I tuned in the radio and found out the temperature was eighty-four degrees. If it reached eighty-five, it would break a record. There was rain in the forecast, too, the percentage growing higher through the night into the early morning. As I drove the sun would break through the cloud cover for a few seconds, intermittent with the rumbling of thunder off in the distance. There were small, unfoamy ruffles cluttering the surface of the gray-green lake water. As I got closer to the north shore, raindrops would dapple the windshield occasionally, but never enough for me to turn on the wipers.

I drove into Covington and through the back streets to the entrance of the Cotton estate. I started to turn in to the shelled drive, but some sixth sense directed me to park beyond it and not announce my arrival.

I walked onto the grounds, cut across the tennis court, went around the pool and behind the pool house. I had no idea why I was being so circumspect, but before I left the cover of the pool house and went out into the open, I took a long look at the larger house. It nestled like a jewel in the lush purple velvet of profusely blooming azaleas.

Everything was still and quiet; the house looked closed up. I kept close to the camellia bushes at the edge of the property and went down the slope of land to the lagoon. I circled it and came up on the left side of the house. There was nothing to see, no lights and no movement through any of the downstairs windows.

I stepped onto the veranda and went around to the back. The garage was below me, down another, smaller slope of land. I wanted to see if there were any cars in it, but not before I checked out the smaller structure on the right of the house.

I crouched down and dashed across the twenty-five or thirty feet of grass that separated the two buildings to an oak tree that sheltered the little one. From there the two sets of French doors leading into the cottage from a narrow, empty patio were visible. One pair of doors was open.

No one was in the room. I could see the corner of a bed with a white spread on it, and a chiffonier of dark wood with a small mirror on top. Off to one side of it was an old-fashioned floor-length mirror, an oval glass tilted back a bit in its elaborate curved stand. On the other side was a door leading to a front room.

I waited and watched for several minutes. I was about to leave the oak tree and venture inside when I heard the amplified sound of a needle jumping off a record. Someone put it back on, and a rather slow reggae beat wafted through the door.

There was a flash of white in the inside doorway, and Quiro floated into the bedroom. He stopped, executed a short, neat dance step, turned twice, then moved foward with the music until he was in front of the oval mirror. His timing was perfect, his every movement graceful, without exaggeration, his footwork flawless, dangerously complicated looking in the stiletto high heels he wore on his feet. He was also wearing Paula Cotton's bared-shoulder, white-sequined gown.

The white dress set off his *café au lait* skin spectacularly. As his dipping and swaying and dancing became more fervent, his skin took on a sheen, a richly oiled glow that was more sensational than a thousand flashing sequins. I couldn't help thinking it: In that dress, the way he moved his straight, slim, flat-chested body, he exuded more sexuality than Paula Cotton in all of her expensive alabaster perfection ever could. I thought of her outrage if she knew he was prancing and sweating in her costly designer gown. White-hot outrage.

Another song ended, and Quiro hurried back into the front room. He returned carrying a silver candlestick, stood in front of the mirror, held the candlestick up to his mouth, and lip-synched to a Billie Holiday record. He would raise his free arm over his head, then clutch it to his chest, causing his exposed back muscles to flex and ripple under his smooth, shiny skin. Every now and again I could glimpse his tortured or ecstatic face reflected in the mirror.

I have never felt more like a voyeur, and that's saying something given the business I'm in. I wanted to go down to the garage, but I didn't think I could make it without his seeing me. Even if I waited until he changed the record, it would be risky. There was no indication, anyway, that there was anyone else around; what he was doing seemed to be for his own personal pleasure, and even if it wasn't my idea of a good time I figured he had a right to his privacy.

I waited until the record was finished and he left the bedroom, then I went back the way I had come, another loner in the haze.

26

Whistling in the Dark

For the second time that day, I stood in the shadow of a tree and listened.

Lee hadn't been at her office when I got back from across the lake, so I drove up Magazine Street to Audubon Park.

A light wind had blown up, and the leaves on the giant oaks rustled softly. That soft sound was like whispers in the twilight. A chill came over me that riddled my bones with superstition.

The door opened and Lee came out on the small front porch. Her body was tightly wrapped in a white terry cloth robe; her hair was wrapped in a towel. She went to the side of the porch and stared down into the bushes. I came out of the shadows.

"Hi."

She turned around, but not fast like she would have if I'd frightened her. When she said, "Neal," though, it was with relief.

"Looking for something?"

"I'm supposed to get a newspaper delivered, but I think it ends up in the bushes most of the time."

I crossed the lawn to the bushes and found the paper. There were a couple more rotting into the soil. I went to the end of the hedge and stepped up onto the low porch. She held out her hand for the paper, and looked up into my face rather dreamily. Her

162

pupils were large in the gathering darkness. I put my arm across her shoulders, and led her inside.

I closed the door behind us. She dropped the paper on a small table at her side, and stood fixed in front of me, smaller than usual in her bare feet. A fragrant, smoky smell, vaguely familiar, seemed to be coming from her. I bent and kissed her neck. A more perfumy scent lingered there. I lifted my head. The smell was in the apartment, odd, Eastern, the hint of a medicinal potion.

"What's that smell?" I asked.

"I burned some incense earlier."

"Heady," I murmured and bent down again.

"I have to go," she whispered, her lips brushing mine, her arms coming up around my back.

I pushed her robe open and off her shoulders; she moved her arms and with a small, sensual shrug, let the robe fall to the floor.

Sometime later she got up and turned on a lamp. I was sprawled on the futon, smoking a cigarette.

She slipped on a pair of navy-blue trousers. "I was supposed to be at Paula's ten minutes ago," she said. "I left a message for you this afternoon. Didn't you get it?"

I shook my head languidly. "Where's Richard Cotton, Lee?"

"He told her he'd be back tomorrow. He won't tell her where he is." She went to the closet and pulled out a deep-rose silk blouse. "She's quite furious."

"Doesn't he give her any kind of explanation?"

"None. I think he's going to come back tomorrow and end the marriage." She started brushing her hair with long, swift pulls.

I got up and went into the bathroom. "Why do you think that?"

"I don't know. It's just what I think."

I threw some water on half my face, and picked up a towel. "What does she think?"

On the side of the bathtub in a jade-green pot was a stick of incense burned halfway down. I put my nose to it. Jasmine?

Lee came into the bathroom and handed me my clothes. She took out some makeup. "She's thinking about what she should do."

"If it blows?"

She nodded. "One part of her wants to fight it; another wants to be the first to say it's over. Especially the way he's acting now." With a little foam-tipped wand she began applying plum-colored shadow to an eyelid.

"I saw Quiro today," I said.

She looked at me in the mirror. "Where?"

"Across the lake. He was playing dress-up in the gown Paula wore at her party, lip-synching in front of a mirror to Billie Holiday."

The wand stopped mid-stroke. "Life in the country isn't simple anymore, is it," she said.

While she used another wand to make her eyelashes look twice as long, I told her about the rest of the day.

I followed her back into the bedroom, watching how her pants stretched, then loosened over her rear end as she walked. It was fascinating.

"You're sure Quiro didn't see you?" she asked.

"Pretty sure."

She opened a dresser drawer and took out a sweater. "And you really don't think the same person broke into your office and Mr. D.'s place?"

"I don't think so."

She swung the sweater over her shoulders and looped the arms of it around her neck. She checked her watch. "I've got to go, love."

Outside the wind was stronger. I kissed her good-bye under the streetlight, her hair whipping around our faces, and walked across the street to my car.

"Neal," she called to me, her voice pitched high against the wind. I turned from the opened door. She was standing where I'd left her. I imagined the way her body would move if she were to throw a knife across the distance between us. "Be careful," she said.

The wind died momentarily, and came up again to whistle in the dark.

27

Rain

The rain started early the next morning. The night before I'd gone home from Lee's and tried to think about Callahan, Mr. D., Richard, but my brain was in an exhausted stupor, and I'd fallen asleep shortly after nine o'clock. I woke up to the sound of wind howling around the side of the Euclid and rain lashing up against the windows. By ten that morning half the city was under water.

I made it to the office without swimming. In fact, the only problem I had getting downtown was the traffic, which was snarled even where there was no standing water; but any kind of unusual weather in New Orleans causes a traffic jam, and there's a lot of unusual weather in New Orleans.

Gabe hustled over to park the car as I entered the garage at the Père Marquette. I could tell he was energized by the way he spryly hopped off the conveyer belt that brings the attendants to the upper levels of the garage. Also, the toothpick that normally hangs in one place off his lip was moving rapidly from side to side of his mouth.

"Some weather!" he called to someone walking through the garage as he bounded up to my car.

Floods—hurricanes, too—seem to charge up some people, especially if they haven't been or aren't in particular danger of being victimized by the wiles of nature. I remember Mrs. Tim, my parents' next-door neighbor, standing out on her porch just before Hurricane Betsy hit, saying over and over again, "It's *beautiful!* Isn't it *beautiful!*"

Gabe opened the car door for me, and then he saw the bandages on my face. The toothpick stopped its rapid transit while he chewed on it. He started to say something, but changed his mind. "You must be part duck, Mr. Rafferty," he said instead.

"Sitting duck," I replied, and left the car to him.

I was going through the mail when the telephone rang. It was the elusive Mr. Cotton.

"Where've you been, Richard?"

"Thinking," he said. "I've decided not to run for district attorney. I want you to stop looking for anything Solarno might have had on Callahan. There's probably nothing to it anyway."

"I already know what Solarno had on Callahan. The drugs were distributed from the Bucktown Tavern."

He paused about a beat and a half. "Do you have proof?" he asked, not too excited. Desperately hopeful, maybe.

"Not yet. I'm going to find a way to get him."

He actually laughed. "How? He's a very powerful man. He's pulled off a brilliant operation, nabbing those judges, and I would say, very effectively closing down the tavern."

"Yeah, but he's in very deep. I'm pretty sure he had a cop gun down a young kid who was running the drugs and decided to dip into the cache and deal some for himself. You know, the busboy at the tavern."

"And how are you going to make the cop talk? I'm sorry, Neal, but I don't believe there's any way of stopping him."

"There's more. First, Callahan bothered to call me to his office and tell me to lay off. Then my office was broken into and your file was taken. Callahan knows you hired Solarno, Richard. Solarno must have gone to him, and that's when he probably decided to plan the raids, shut down the tavern. And get rid of Marty Solarno."

"And get somebody else to get rid of Marty Solarno. Don't you see? It's all too far away from him. Callahan's too smart. There's no way to get to him."

"There's always a way, some mistake, some chink. I want you to help me find it. I want you to help me build a case against him."

"I can't, Neal. I wanted to get him out of office, but I know that I can't. That's as far as it goes for me."

"Then it should go further," I told him. "Callahan isn't a man who should have a grain of power. If all he did was abuse it by taking a few bribes here and there, maybe I'd be willing to say it wasn't worth the trouble. But he kills people. You know as well as I do that he had Marty Solarno killed."

"Solarno was scum," Richard said, irritated. "And, anyway, you have absolutely no proof that Callahan had anything to do with his murder."

"Has Callahan threatened you? Is that it? Or Paula? Is he threatening your wife?"

"I don't know what you're talking about."

"Have you talked to Callahan, Richard?"

"No."

"Then what is this?" I practically yelled into the phone. "Am I the only person left who believes Callahan should be stopped before he decides someone else should be removed?" I told him how close I'd come to not having this conversation with him.

"Oh God." His voice cracked.

"I need your help, Richard."

"I'm not able to help you." I could hardly hear him.

"Talk to me, Richard. I need you to see this through with me. You set something in motion, and we have to finish it before someone else gets hurt. We have to try."

"I'm a broken man, Neal. My life is falling apart around me. I don't seem to have any control anymore. I didn't want it to come to this. I'm very sorry you were hurt."

I didn't want to hear this kind of whimpering bullshit. I wanted information. "Is there anyone on Callahan's staff or anyone he uses for outside work who has a gravel voice?" I asked him.

"No one I know of. I need to go now, Neal."

"Not yet. I want to know what Christopher Raven was doing inside your house."

"I don't know. I've told you that. I didn't know him."

"You don't know too much. Raven worked at the Bucktown Tavern, too. Another busboy," I said sarcastically.

Dead silence now. Then, "At the tavern?" He was completely, believably incredulous. "How do you know?"

"Mr. D. told me."

"Who?"

"Danny Dideaux. Mr. D.'s Laundry. Don't bother to tell me you don't know *him*. He told me himself that you and Quiro both have been to the laundry. Why didn't you ask him if Solarno had a film?"

He stopped whining and came alive. "That's right. I've been to the laundry and so has Quiro, and Dideaux's a worse piece of filth than Solarno was. I wouldn't ask him for anything. I'm sorry you did. I can tell you've put a lot of time into this, and it's caused you a great deal of trouble. I never should have asked you to do it. Figure out how much time you spent, and I'll write you a check."

Now I lost control. "But you *did* ask me to do it, goddamn it, and I didn't do it for money. I did it because I consider you a friend. I did it for you. And for me, too."

"Please forgive me," he said, and the phone went dead.

I was still fuming an hour later.

28

Come
Live with Me

By three o'clock in the afternoon a lot of the floodwater uptown had subsided. I called Lee's office and got the answering service. When I tried her apartment, I got a recording that the phone was temporarily out of service. It was probably because of all the rain, but I thought I'd better go check.

The streets were full of debris from the storm. Limbs of trees had been knocked down by the wind, and wires hung from poles or lay coiled on the sidewalk like snakes ready to strike. At one point I had to circle a block because a large tree had been split almost in half, its length blocking the street when it fell.

I drove into the side street next to Lee's that dead-ended at the park and pulled up behind her Mustang. Ripples of dirt lined the concrete like sand rippled by the surf. Lakes of water stood in the park, the water level too high, the earth too saturated to absorb them. More dirt made gritty sounds under my shoes as I stepped up on the porch. It was obvious what had happened. It seems like every time the rains come, another part of town goes under.

Lee came to the door dressed in the same clothes she'd had on the night before, except that she was barefoot and the bottoms of her pantlegs were wet. Her face was expressionless, but her skin more cream than honey, and her eyes, yellow in the filtered light that is sometimes a part of the aftermath of such weather, were sad. The skin around them looked bruised in contrast to her pale cheeks.

The floor of the apartment was much the same as the floor of the porch. I could see along the baseboards how high the water had risen. It was only a couple of inches, but enough to cause a lot of damage, especially the way the place was furnished. The futon that was her sofa had a dirty water mark around it; the cushions surrounding the lacquered table were sodden.

I put my arms around her. "I'm sorry, baby," I said.

She leaned against me a minute. When we separated, she said, "It doesn't matter so much," but she wouldn't look at me. She started walking toward the back. "There was only one thing I really cared about."

I followed her into the bedroom. At the foot of the futon was a small prayer rug, thin as silk with age. We both stared down at it, at the delicate colors of the vegetable dye all running together.

"It was my father's," she said. "He carried it with him for years." I could see her eyes blinking rapidly. "It wasn't supposed to happen here, was it?" she asked, but she wasn't really asking me.

She straightened her shoulders. "He warned me about being sentimental. Now there's nothing left to be sentimental about. I'm sure I'll be relieved."

I bit my tongue—I wasn't the right guy to be talking to about sentimentality.

There was a mop leaning against a wall in the bathroom. When I'd arrived, she had apparently been getting up the last of the water with it. She picked it up and wrung it out, then wiped the tiles a few more times.

I pushed down on the futon with the palm of my hand. A little water squished out underneath the place I pushed. "Your bed is ruined," I said inanely.

"It doesn't matter," she said once again. "There's a smaller one in a storage closet upstairs. I can use that until I replace it."

Together we squeezed as much water out of it as we could and lugged it out of the apartment. Lee was as remote and inscrutable as a Buddhist monk while we worked, which wasn't for long.

"I appreciate your help," she told me, "but I'd like to be alone for a while."

"Will you come stay with me tonight?" I asked.

"Maybe. I've got a few things to tie up first. Maybe after that. I'm not promising."

"The Cottons?"

She nodded. "They had a terrible fight this morning. Paula called me afterward and asked me to take her across the lake. It's been an exhausting day." But she didn't look exhausted. She had that quiet readiness about her, like she was up to handling anything, and could handle it alone. I supposed, though, she was holding all of the emotion inside her very carefully, not about to let the smallest amount leak out until she'd gotten done what she had to do.

I felt bad for her, for her aloneness, for all our aloneness when we're faced with loss, no matter how much comfort is offered. I left wanting to insist that she come to me after she did whatever she had to do for Paula Cotton and her loss, but I knew better.

My hand crunched the piece of newspaper when I got in the car. I had carried it around with me for a couple of days, but I'd more or less forgotten about it. I picked it up now, though, and looked at the listing for the apartment in the Garden District.

There was a pay phone in front of a Time-Saver on Prytania Street. I hoped that the apartment hadn't already been taken. An elderly-sounding lady answered the phone and told me I could come look at it now if I wanted to.

It was on Philip Street, the renovated carriage house behind the mansion the lady lived in. It hadn't been taken because the rent was obnoxious, but I figured it wasn't much more than what Lee and I were paying together. For the price, you could probably get a four-bedroom house in another part of town, but it was close to our offices, and set back a nice distance from the main house. And the Garden District didn't flood—not yet.

Downstairs there was a kitchen big enough for the two of us, a living room, and another room for the weights. Upstairs the two rooms were airy and full of windows. I looked out of them into the treetops. I thought Lee would like it there. I wanted to show it to her in the morning. I was sure she'd offer a lot of resistance, and I knew that her reasons would be good, but I wanted to convince her that we should give it a shot. I wanted to know what it felt like not to be alone.

The lady was too well bred to snort derisively at my occupation. Instead she asked me for two personal references, and let me have a glance up her nostrils. I gave her Maurice's and Richard's names. When she heard the name Cotton, her nose stopped trying to be the first human parts satellite. Actually I liked her—she didn't talk my ear off, she didn't say anything about noise, and she didn't ask me about my face. She said it would be okay if I dropped a check off first thing in the morning.

The one problem was that I had to get through the night.

29

The Trade-off

All day long I'd wondered if Mr. D. would get the message I'd put out on the street. When I hit the Euclid just before five o'clock, the phone was ringing off the hook.

"Goddamn," Uncle Roddy snapped, "don't you ever check your answerin' service?"

"I've been gone less than two hours!"

"I gotta body here," he said, supremely irritated. "I gotta feeling you know who it is." He told me to get myself over to the Seventeenth Street Canal pumping station. Now.

The surging waters had topped the canal at Palmetto Street and run down to flood out homes in the area between Palmetto and Airline Highway. On the other side of the canal, though, is Metairie Ridge, which was high and dry. I followed the canal along Orpheum Street, across Metairie Road, to where a levee keeps the water back. At the end of the levee the canal widened out to a large pool. On the other side was the pumping station. I parked at the side of the levee because of all the police vehicles further on, and walked down a narrow strip of asphalt to the station. He was lying on a stretch of grass, away from the action of the rotating filters that churned noisily in the water, removing the trash and tossing it to a space above at the side of the station. He had on the same polyester shirt, but he'd lost his shoes, to the canal, I guessed, where they would be the only kind of reptile that

173

could survive in the slimy, murky depths of the bottom mud. His collarbone and hairless chest were exposed, but instead of being sinewy and tough, he seemed juvenile now. There was a knife wound in his too white, too bony ribs.

Uncle Roddy limped slowly to where I knelt at the side of the body.

"Your friend at the motel?" he asked over the grind and churn of the filters.

Uncle Roddy amazed me sometimes. I stood up. "How'd you know?"

"Friends in vice," he said, and I didn't know if he was trying to be funny or was just still irritated. "We know the confiscated films were his."

Fonte had sauntered up, chewing gum so ferociously that his jowls were puffed from exertion. "You shoulda let us go get him, Rafferty."

I wished I had, but I'd be damned if I was going to say so in front of Fonte. Uncle Roddy motioned to the guys with the stretcher. We walked away from Mr. D.'s body and all the noise of the water being filtered and sucked by the pumps.

"Why didn't you go back to the motel right away?" Uncle Roddy asked.

"I went to the hospital."

"After that." Not quite a bark, but he was definitely still irritated.

"I went home to get some clothes that weren't full of blood. I was tired and hurting and I figured he was safe at the motel." It was the truth, but I hated saying it.

"Hard to leave the little nest, isn't it," Fonte said and let go with a humor-filled snort.

I wanted to punch him out.

I would like to say that if Lee hadn't come over I wouldn't have gone back downtown, anyway, but it probably isn't so. It doesn't matter, I still wanted to slug Fonte.

Tight-lipped, I said to Uncle Roddy, "By the time I got my face sewn up he was already gone."

Fonte answered with, "How come everybody you talk to gets dead and you stay alive?"

I punched him square in his gum-swelled jaw. He staggered back and Uncle Roddy let out a roar that made the noise behind us sound like music boxes.

Uncle Roddy's roars subdue me, but Fonte was undaunted. Rubbing on his jaw, he started, "That does it. Assault of an officer—"

This time Uncle Roddy's roar was decipherable. "Let it go!" He glared at Fonte, then at me. "If you two wanna duke it out, do it away from me. Got it?" He waited until we both nodded, then he asked me, "Do you know what Dideaux's deal was with Callahan?"

"He told me he talked to Yastovich. It was Yastovich who told him to get films to the Bucktown Tavern. Why don't you ask Callahan?"

"I'm on my way to do that, wise guy. Callahan called in about fifteen minutes ago. He said he just found Yastovich's body."

A drink was what I needed to calm the shaky feeling I was left with after punching Fonte. I wouldn't have had that feeling if I'd been able to punch him enough.

I sat at the bar in a place on Metairie Road called the Metry Café and thought. Solarno was one thing, but it made no sense for Callahan to kill Mr. D. My own arguments to Mr. D. still held as far as I was concerned. Mr. D. had cooperated, so why would Callahan be searching his premises and watching him? Also, Mr. D. was a penny-ante operator who kept to himself, and even if he'd found a way to extort money from Callahan, there were too many ways that a powerful district attorney could have stopped him if he'd chosen to stop him. He could have had Leonard Yastovich set him up, but instead Yastovich had used Mr. D. to get information crucial to the success of the raids. It was more likely that Callahan had some evidence against Mr. D. that he had used to strike a bargain with the two-bit porno prince—I didn't see Mr. D. being a willing informant. The more I thought about it the more convinced I became that just as there were two different people breaking into my office and Mr. D.'s apartment, there were two different murderers.

There weren't too many people left who knew very much about Chance Callahan. There was a cop who had shot and killed a young kid who'd been tagged a "known and possibly dangerous drug dealer." The cop was being protected by Callahan. There were the owners of the Bucktown Tavern. Maybe there was a chance they'd talk, but they also had plenty of money to hire slick lawyers. Thanks to Callahan. And there was Richard Cotton.

Why was Richard so desperate to get something on Callahan? What reckless things had he done when he was younger that he didn't like to talk about? Why was he being so secretive about where he'd been the last couple of days? There was also the word he'd used on the phone that morning to describe Solarno—scum.

When Chance Callahan called me to his office, he may have wanted to know if Solarno had something tangible, but somehow I didn't think that was the only reason he'd called me, maybe not even the most important one. What the hell was it?

There was another thing—Mr. D. had said that both Richard and Quiro had been to the laundry, but that didn't mean they'd been there to rent films. What if Mr. D. had been blackmailing Richard—about his reckless youth, or, try this, about why Christopher Raven was in Richard's house? That would be a way for Mr. D. to cut his losses in payoffs and confiscated films.

Something was going on with Richard Cotton, and it wasn't that a Garden District aristocrat liked to break out of his staid existence on the uppercrust once in a while to drink beer with a bunch of Yahoos in Bucktown.

It took me about twenty-five minutes to get to the Cottons' house. During those minutes I asked over and over the only question that had any real significance: Where was Lee? And the only answer I could come up with was that she was in a house with a murderer. I prayed that it wasn't a house that was nearly forty-five minutes away on several isolated acres of land in Covington. Even a karate expert couldn't catch a knife that was thrown at her back.

When I got to the house, the Mercedes was in the driveway. A police car was pulled up behind it. Another one and an unmarked car were parked on the street. So was the black Mustang. When I saw it, the muscles in my stomach knotted. I ran up the steps to the front door.

Fonte let me in.

"Where's Lee?" I demanded.

"In the back." I started past him, but he blocked my way. "You're too late," he said, and my stomach started going to pieces. "Too late," he repeated maliciously.

I went around him, pushing him to the side. He put a restraining hand on my arm. I slung it off. After that, he just let me go.

I went down the hallway, past the dining room, and into the den. A uniformed officer stood to the side of the doorway to the library. It was Gaudet, one of the officers who'd been there the night Raven burned up in the fireplace. He nodded to me, and I stepped inside the large, book-lined room.

They were talking softly. She had pulled a chair up to the sofa so she was directly in front of him. He leaned toward her so their heads were close together, his back to me. I stepped a little further into the room so I could hear them. Lee glanced at me; Quiro didn't bother to turn around.

Quiro said in his soft, rhythmic speech, "You know why I followed you, Lee. I had to make sure you didn't want to hurt Richard."

She nodded. "I know. And the phone calls to Paula, the scratching at the doors . . ."

"I want her to leave," he said with some vehemence. "I tried to scare her to make her leave. She's no good for him."

"But she's his wife. That's his decision."

He shook his head. "She makes him feel guilty for being what he is. He doesn't want her. He doesn't want any woman."

She nodded again, conciliatory. "Did he want the man who died here in the fireplace?"

"No! Raven was an employee, but I knew he was into dope. I

got him to get me some stuff and he made Richard pay for it all over again. That made Richard angry at me. That night I told Raven never do that again. Raven said if I told Richard not to pay, he would put stuff in the house and call the cops. He said he would tell everyone what Richard really was, starting with his wife and his law partners. He said he could get Richard plenty of trouble. He laughed at him. All they want is his money."

"Who?"

"No one anymore. You got rid of the first one; I got rid of the other one."

"Mr. D.?"

"Yes. Richard never should have given him anything. He should have told me a long time ago what Danny was up to. I told Richard to let Chance Callahan take care of Danny, but Richard said Danny wouldn't ask for any more. Then he calls Richard and tells him Callahan is after him, that he needs more money to go away for good. But Chance Callahan wasn't after Danny. I was." He laughed, a strange, low laugh that was more like a cry than a laugh, a strangled sound caught in the throat. I'd heard a laugh similar to it come from a retarded child once.

He shifted abruptly. I took a step forward, alarmed that he was going to try to hurt Lee, but he turned his body, straightening it so he was nearly lying on his side. "I want to give you something, Lee." His cuffed hands struggled to get into one of his pants pockets. He sat up, holding something I couldn't see out to her. "I can't use it anymore. I want you to have it."

She made no move to take whatever it was. His shoulders jerked as he thrust it at her. "Go on. Take it. They won't search you."

That's when it all hooked up in my mind, what I'd smelled in her apartment, that same sweet, smoky, vaguely medicinal odor I'd gotten a brief whiff of in the house across the lake the first time I'd gone there, a smell not quite like anything I'd ever smelled before. I was willing to bet it was part of the stash of opium that was found in the house of the gunned-down black kid who had worked at the Bucktown Tavern.

She took it from him and put it in her purse. A wave of repulsion came over me at the thought that the two of them might have smoked opium together. I was angry, too. And there was something else worming its way deep inside me that hurt much more than the anger or the repulsion.

He was making a trade-off. "I want you to tell Paula that she should leave. Will you do that, Lee?"

She didn't answer him. They sat looking at each other, and I stood behind them, my legs like concrete columns.

Fonte came into the room. "Time to go," he said. He took Quiro by the arm.

When Quiro turned around he was no longer the cocksure, dancerlike man he had been. His entire carriage was different. The smooth brown skin of his face was puffy, like he'd been crying, or was about to, because his deep, round eyes were glistening. As he passed me, he said, "Take care of that face, boss."

My guardian angel. My guardian angel was a psycho killer.

Lee and I followed him and Fonte to the front of the house. When he got to the stairway, Quiro stopped, holding strong against Fonte, who tried to keep him moving. He looked up at the stairs, and the smallest drop of liquid fell out of his right eye. He turned to me and said, "Tell Richard good-bye for me," and then Fonte led him away.

30

The Standoff

We watched Quiro leave, then Lee went to the rear of the house to get her purse.

Fonte came back inside with Gaudet, who stationed himself at the front door. I was still standing at the foot of the stairway. Fonte swaggered down the hallway toward me, a slow, practiced, police-on-the-beat walk. There was a bluish stain on his jawline where I'd hit him.

"Rankin's with Callahan?" I asked.

"That's right. This one's my show, Rafferty. Your girlfriend called me," he stated smugly. He dropped his voice to a low snarl. "Time for you to say bye-bye."

No way. I stood my ground, waiting for Lee. I could hear her coming up behind me.

Fonte's face broke into a wide, friendly smile. He spoke over my shoulder to her. "I need a statement, Lee."

"Will tomorrow morning do, Phil? I'm hardly able to think I'm so tired." He nodded, a curt dip of his head. Lee said, "And thanks for giving me some time with Quiro."

"Consider it an even exchange—I'll need something from you someday."

The piece of sleaze, trying to get his hooks into her. If I stayed much longer, I was going to start pounding him, not that she needed any help from me.

She said, "Another collar, maybe?"

His jaw flexed, vacant without the usual wad of gum.

There was one more thing I hoped she'd say to him, but she didn't. Maybe he was just too repulsive to talk to.

She started out, me behind her.

Gaudet opened the door for us, and we stepped out into the muggy night air left by the rain.

It was dark and quiet in the land of the rich and staid. The tall houses made shadows laced by the treetops. In the house across the street, through elegant, tied-back curtains, the perfectly furnished living room was exposed, perfectly lit to show off high-priced artwork, arrangements of fresh-cut flowers, and the silver ribbons of the burglar alarm system framing the windows. No one was in the room. I had a sudden longing for the treeless, bawdy streets of the Channel where the way people live is not on show all the time, where the demands and problems of having money don't exist. That's not to say there aren't other problems, but they weren't on my mind right then.

We walked past a confederate jasmine vine growing up the lamppost in the front yard. The sweet smell of it filled my nostrils and nearly gagged me. I didn't think I'd ever be able to smell jasmine or anything sweet like that again without it setting off my gag reflex.

"Your place?" Lee asked, and part of me wanted to forget it, but the biggest part of me couldn't.

I waited until we were out on the sidewalk, away from the house. I stopped walking and said, "You forgot to give the opium to Fonte, Lee."

She had taken a step beyond me. Turning swiftly, her brown hair swinging, she faced me squarely.

"Don't tell me I didn't see what Quiro gave you." I was keeping in mind that Maurice had said she could have been a great trial lawyer, and, also, that she didn't like assumptions. "I didn't have to see it. I know what it is, and you didn't give it to Fonte."

"I didn't forget," she said.

"Where I come from, smoking opium is considered a vice. So is lying."

"I have never lied to you, Neal."

"The smell that was in your apartment yesterday was the same thing I smelled in the house across the lake once, and it wasn't incense."

"I did burn incense—while I smoked."

We were talking quietly up to this point, but when she said that, I thought she was cutting a pretty fine distinction, and I was ready to say so—pointedly and heatedly. But she was saying, her voice soft and low, yet clear, "I don't have to tell you all my secrets just because we're lovers. I prefer to smoke alone."

"But you don't always. I guess smoking with Quiro was the reason you were able to crack him wide open." I could feel anger rising, filling up my chest.

"No, Neal, I would never have smoked with Quiro."

The streetlight that was several feet behind her was making her eyes burn yellow, not like they had in the firelight, but the way they had on that first night we'd stayed together. The anger slid back like a snake into its hole.

"Then why did he use it to make a trade-off with you?"

"Because when Paula Cotton and I went to the Covington house this morning, I smelled it, and I told him I knew he was smoking opium. He didn't have to ask how I knew."

"You should have given it to Fonte."

"Why? Because that's what you would have done?" It was a simple question; she wasn't attacking me.

"Because it's the right thing to do."

"Have you never done anything that wasn't right?" Another simple question, not cynical or sarcastic, not a question I would have liked to answer. "I'm not like you, Neal."

I wanted to put my hands on her shoulders, shake her maybe, but that was no way to convince Lee Diamond. "Don't you see that taking the stuff from Quiro makes you vulnerable?"

"If I thought that, I'd have given it to Fonte." Her eyes seared my face. "Does your knowing I took it make me vulnerable? Would you feel differently about this if I'd told you I liked to smoke? Would you still think I was wrong?"

Her questions were maddening. My chest was beginning to feel full again. "I'm surprised you would ask questions that require an assumption. The fact is that's not how it happened." I didn't say it as nastily as I might have. There was something about her quietness and reserve, her control, that was rather compelling.

"I think you've been very unscrupulous," I said. "If Quiro didn't confess to you while he was in an opium dream, then you used information you got from me."

"You had the information before I did."

That put me right on the edge of being furious. "What the hell is this—some kind of competition?"

I felt only a moment's relief when her eyes left my face while she shook her head.

"When I brought Quiro back from across the lake this afternoon, I didn't know Danny Dideaux was dead. I didn't know that until I heard the evening news, after you left this afternoon. Quiro was with Richard Cotton. By the time I realized what had happened, I thought Cotton might have tried to get him out of the country. I gave him plenty of time to do that while I was busy shedding a few tears over what I lost in the flood."

"So you called Fonte and had him meet you here?" She nodded. "Why not Rankin?"

"I called him first. He was out."

I was ready to buy it, but I wasn't ready to let her off the hook.

"The thing is, Lee, I told you about the death threat I found in Danny's apartment, and I told you about Quiro playing Billie Holiday in Paula's dress. But you didn't tell me you knew Richard Cotton is a homosexual."

"I was keeping a client's confidence. Anyway, he's your friend— I thought you knew that."

"Another assumption, Miss Diamond. He's kept it well hidden. I doubt that many people know, but you did."

"I knew because Paula told me. When she hired me, she wasn't worried about other women, she was worried about other men. And she was embarrassed, humiliated. I took the case because she'd received several threats over the phone."

"You didn't tell me that either."

"They stopped for a while after Raven died."

"That's another thing—after Delahoussaye told you Raven was bisexual, you must have at least suspected there was some sort of tie between him and Richard."

Any appeasement she'd been trying for was over with now. In a much colder, more detached tone she said, "I wasn't working with you on that case, Neal, and I don't like having to defend myself this way. Anything I didn't tell you, I chose not to tell you, just as there are things you choose not to tell me."

"Only out of fear that you'll call me sentimental or self-indulgent."

We had reached an impasse. She asked me if I still wanted her to come over, but I didn't. I didn't really believe she wanted to be with me either. When she got in the car and drove away, she may have been sad, but her detachment, her self-containment, was so complete that it was hard to tell.

I walked down the street to my car, and Myra was on my mind. And maybe from force of habit whenever I thought about her, or because I'd been thinking about the Channel, the old man, too. What was it the old man had said, that when all else fails, they cry? It wasn't like that at all. None of it had been like he said. You don't fight with a woman like Lee Diamond. She gives you no ground. You don't raise your voice to her, or she'll leave. If she cries, she cries alone.

You don't try to save a woman like Lee Diamond, and you don't try to possess her, either. If you try to help her or protect her, you're only competing with her own survival instincts. Maybe I'd gotten too used to trying to save Myra so I could have her to myself. I'd tried to win Myra, but I wasn't competing with her because of her profession, or even with the other men she slept with. I had been competing with something inside myself, and that competition, I had to admit, had started a long time ago—at home.

31

A Whiter Shade of Pale

I parked in the next block down from the Cottons' and waited until I saw Fonte and Gaudet leave. When I saw them brake at Prytania, I proceeded slowly up the street and parked in front of the house. I took my time getting out of the car, looking up at the dim light behind the curtains in the second-story windows, but I hurried past the jasmine holding my breath.

I had to ring the bell three times before he answered. His lean, handsome face was gaunt, sunken below the high contour of the cheekbones. It looked as if he'd lost some weight, and gave me an idea of how he might age, becoming angular if he got too thin, and maybe not so debonair as he'd been when he was thirty, but aristocratic to the last.

His light blue eyes were on my bandage, which had been changed and was not quite as bulky, but my eye was still covered. The sight of me made him wilt some more.

"I want to talk to you, Richard."

He held the door open, then led me down what was becoming a familiar path in his house to the library.

"Would you like a drink?" he asked.

"No." I was fed up with vices of all kinds.

I watched him get a bottle of Warre's port out of a cabinet under the bookshelves, a small crystal glass on a stem from the art deco cabinet, and pour some wine for himself. He put the bottle on the desk, and the glass next to it, untouched. He stood at the side of the desk; I stood behind the sofa, my thighs pressed up against its back, my hands in my pockets.

"I hope you, too, don't need to be convinced that I had no part in what Quiro has done," he said.

No, I needed to be convinced that there was a damn good reason why I was never going to look the same again, but all I said again was, "No."

He nodded, and his Adam's apple bobbed in his throat a couple of times. He picked up the glass of port and drank it all at once. I made a mental note never to do that in front of anyone again, never to appear to be that weak and vulnerable and dependent, no matter how much my nerves needed to be calmed.

I said to him, "I'm wondering, did you think I wouldn't like you anymore if I knew you were a homosexual?"

He was rolling the bottom of the glass on his palm. "I thought it was possible," he said.

"It would have shocked me a lot less for you to tell me you were gay than to tell me you'd hired Marty Solarno."

He gave a short, sardonic laugh. "I guess so. The funny thing is, Solarno never tried to use my secret life against me. Some people have, and not all of them were straight, either."

"They could only do that because they know you're terrified of being found out."

He nodded agreement. "It would cause Paula a great deal of embarrassment. It would change my life radically, and I'm not sure enough about what I want yet to make a change like that."

"You mean running for public office?"

"That's just one thing. There's my law practice, which is successful partly because my name is Cotton, because I'm the Colonel's son. The Colonel was more than a man, you know. He was a symbol of the old values, of tradition, of the establishment which is like royalty in this town.

"And the thing is that part of me likes all that, and likes being part of it, the status, the respect, maybe even the envy, all of the things that the other part of me hates and is disgusted by. Sometimes I want to just chuck it all, and then sometimes I want to have children to pass it all on to. It's a conflict I can't seem to reconcile. Just when I think I've seen my way clear to go one way, the other side starts pulling and tugging and won't let me. So I end up leading this double life that I know is more difficult and more painful than just making a decision."

"Are you sure you're not confusing what's expected of you with what you want?"

He spread his hands out in front of him. "Don't you see? I want it all."

"Even being district attorney? It seems to me that would make life very complicated."

"No, I thought it would be a way to uncomplicate things, a way of deciding some things without arbitrarily making a decision. It was tossing it to the Fates." He poured another glass of port. "But I began to realize that was only a way of justifying and camouflaging the real motivation—I cared a lot less about being district attorney than I did about beating Chance Callahan."

I came around the sofa. "Was Callahan your first male lover?" I asked.

He took a sip of port and looked at me over the glass. "You really want to get down to it, don't you, Neal? He was the first I cared anything about. He was fascinating, witty, sophisticated, experienced, exciting. Things happened when Callahan was around, and he could juggle two lives with his eyes closed and one hand tied behind his back. He enjoyed doing it, said it made him feel very wicked. When I was with him, I wasn't the scourge of the earth. I, too, was fascinating and exciting."

"Who said you were the scourge of the earth?"

"My father. He said all homosexuals were the scourge of the earth."

"How did he find out?"

He tried to laugh, but he grimaced instead. "I told him. I thought we were so much alike. He was my hero. I was the hero's perfect son. I thought I could tell him. But it meant I wasn't perfect anymore; it meant we weren't alike. It made him sick, sick at the sight of me. No yelling, no screaming; he didn't even want to talk to me. You know why he thought, *publicly* thought, it was so great that I wanted to go into the district attorney's office? Because he didn't want me at the bank."

I felt acutely sorry for him, but at the same time I couldn't help realizing that everything I'd done, no matter what I'd told the old man, about Myra, about Angelesi, he still wanted me to be a cop. The irony of it was I hated that he did. I didn't have his stamp of approval, right?

"So you sought refuge with Callahan. Then what?"

"After a while I began to see how evil he really was. I was too young to understand the force of his ruthlessness, but I could feel it."

I walked over to the bookshelves and sat on the edge of a cabinet in the row underneath them. "And eventually you decided you wanted to get Callahan. But something happened before that. I would guess Callahan found a way to use your sexual preference against you even though his is the same. How?"

"That's just your guess."

I lifted myself off the cabinet. "I want an explanation, Richard."

He was bringing his drink to his mouth. He put it down. "I don't believe that I *owe* you any kind of explanation." Very high-handed, heir-apparent bullshit. I could see that he and Callahan must have been quite a pair.

"If not an explanation, what then? Are you going to whip out your checkbook?" He reddened. "Maybe if you'd given me an explanation from the beginning, *this* wouldn't have happened." I put a finger on my face next to the bandage.

"Please." All of a sudden he slammed his fist down on the desk. "Don't you think I feel guilty?" he shouted. "Everyone wants me to feel guilty, my father, my wife. The only reason I got married was because he wanted me to. He had a rotten marriage. My mother turned into a drunk because of it. Is that what he wanted for me? Revenge? Why couldn't he just accept the way I am?"

"Why couldn't *you* accept the way you are? Why did you feel like you had to keep hiding it just because it didn't please your father?"

"Is that your answer to everything? Tell the world and the problem will go away? Are you going to deny the hypocrisy of this town's attitude toward gays, how much fun it is to watch the queers put on their Mardi Gras extravaganzas, go to their balls, their bars, their parties, their restaurants, but don't go to their law offices, don't allow them any real respect or social prominence. Don't give them anything that's reserved for the righteous, God-approved heterosexuals. Because what they're good for is to provide a little local color. God help you if you're gay and not artistic."

"Not everyone feels that way."

"Well, let's just say I was talking about my part of town. You want to tell me about yours?"

The way he said that, so arrogant, so down the goddamn nose, I snapped. "No, I don't want to talk about my part of town, I don't want to talk about gays, I don't want to talk about your guilt feelings. I want to know what Callahan has on you, why you were so desperate to get something on him that you hired Christopher Raven and Marty Solarno."

He went behind the desk and sat down, to put a solid piece of mahogany between us, I guessed. "I was Angelesi's bagman. I didn't know it," he said, then he dismissed that statement with a flip of the hand. "I sort of knew it, after a while. I dummied up to play the game, and because Callahan approved of what I was doing." A muscle at the corner of his mouth jumped. "They made video tapes of me making pickups, one of me at an all-male sex party. Callahan's still got them and he's vengeful enough to use them. I wanted something so there'd at least be a stalemate."

"But Quiro told Lee Diamond that you should have let Callahan take care of Mr. D."

"I've never told anyone about those tapes, not even Quiro. I was too humiliated by my own stupidity. Danny knew about my relationship with Callahan and started hitting me for money after

I left the D.A.'s office, not too often, but when Quiro found out about it, he thought I ought to tell Callahan what Danny was up to."

"Why didn't you?"

His thin lips curved in a mirthless smile. "As a matter of fact, I did. A long time ago. Callahan was very amused by Mr. D.'s resourcefulness. He reminded me that there were worse things Mr. D. could know about. Callahan, of course, is always safe because he's Mr. District Attorney. That's one reason I wanted to get him out of that office."

"Did Christopher Raven apply personally for the job?"

He raked his hand through his hair. "I was a fool, all right? I couldn't believe it when you told me he was at the Bucktown Tavern—I'm paying him for information about Callahan and he's on Callahan's dope payroll. At least he had a few laughs before he died. And Callahan, he must laugh himself silly—the uptown lawyer and his Bucktown clients, a bunch of chumps having dinner and drinking beer in the middle of a drug operation. It makes me crazy, that bastard Raven, selling drugs to Quiro."

"You don't remember him from the D.A.'s office?" He said he didn't. "He became a narcotics informant, until Callahan needed him. How'd you get on to him?"

"The same way you did," he said.

"Mr. D.?"

"Mr. D-vine. I tried to get some return on the money I was giving him. I asked him first. He gave me Raven."

Well, you had to give Mr. D. some credit. After all, he had his scruples (and a healthy fear of Callahan, I'm sure), but he wasn't one to miss an opportunity for a kickback. Or a few good laughs, either.

Richard said, "The next thing I knew, Raven was coming to me to pay for Quiro's dope. That's when I told Quiro about Danny. I told him he was giving both of them more ways to get money out of me. I told him it had to be stopped. What in God's name did he think I meant?"

"He didn't kill Danny right away, Richard." No, and I

wondered if Quiro would have killed anyone if Raven hadn't died after falling in the fireplace. It was too much to think about.

"He did it after I sent him to the laundry with more money the week before Mardi Gras," Richard said. "Danny must have wanted the films he was going to lose in the raids covered. I told Quiro I couldn't stand going there one more time."

And Quiro must have told Richard that he killed Danny, and that's when Richard disappeared for a few days trying to decide what to do. The only decisive action he'd been able to take, apparently, was to pull out of the D.A.'s race. I saw no point in talking to him about that. I said, "I guess Callahan called me to his office to see if I was Solarno's replacement. He wanted to know how much you'd told me." And I was such a logical choice, too. The thought didn't make me happy. I went on. "I'm surprised Callahan and Angelesi let you out of their clutches after going to the trouble to make the tapes, or was that just for insurance? It seems to me that a man with your various qualifications would be hard to replace."

It was a slur, I admit.

"If I was worried about getting out, it was only for a little while. Because *you* came along." He made that statement with some deprecation, and enjoyed it. "When you lit into Angelesi, Callahan saw his big chance. It was quite amazing to watch him play both ends the way he did. He had Angelesi believing he was working on his side. Then he got Solarno and turned him into the star witness at Angelesi's trial. He used every allegation you made against Angelesi. While all that was going on, I eased myself out of the district attorney's office."

Not every allegation. There was one Callahan hadn't used, and that was Myra Ledet's murder. That would have been his hold over Solarno, that and the promise of sharing some power.

"I found Myra's gold star in Solarno's apartment," I said out loud, but even as I said it I knew that if Solarno had killed Myra, then there would have been no reason for Callahan to fear anything Solarno had on him.

"You didn't tell me," Richard said.

"You didn't ask," I answered automatically, but then I knew why he had never asked: He had never expected me to find anything in Solarno's apartment to link Solarno to Myra.

I shaded my eyes with one hand while a shock wave created an ungodly disturbance in my brain. All this time I'd been thinking that Solarno found out about the Bucktown Tavern and told Callahan. But that wasn't it at all. That wasn't what Solarno knew.

Solarno had never tried to kill me not only because he and Callahan needed me, but also because he wasn't a murderer. He hadn't known who the gold star belonged to—what he told Danny Dideaux about the way he'd gotten it was the truth. I wondered if Callahan unloaded the star on Solarno because it amused him to do so, or if it was another insurance policy—his word against the word of a man whose name was a joke around town. And then something else occurred to me: What if it was the gold star Solarno was going to show Richard? If Richard told Solarno about the murder, Solarno must have figured he was set up for life. After all, he didn't want much, just to get back on Callahan's staff. But Callahan didn't like anyone knowing anything about him that he didn't want known. Callahan would have told Yastovich not to remove anything of value from Solarno's apartment. It was a coincidence, one of those coincidences that private eyes aren't supposed to believe in, that either Yastovich or the guy with the knife couldn't resist taking a porno film. They were probably rifling my office while I was in Callahan's to see if I'd gotten my hands on the star, a good reason for Callahan to call me.

Callahan's voice reverberated inside my skull: "You, Rafferty. Even what you think you know, you don't."

Two steps put me at Richard's side. I grabbed a handful of his shirt front, lifted him up, kicked out the chair he was sitting in, and slammed him down in it again, pushing his neck over the back of it. "You knew Solarno didn't kill Myra," I shouted at him. I picked his head up with his collar and slammed it down a second time. "You baited me. You deliberately set me up, talking about Angelesi and how I went after him so I would go to Solarno's apartment and get your dirt for you when you knew the whole time that Callahan killed Myra. You knew it, and you knew it could get me killed, too." My fist was pushing into his throat. "It came damned close," I yelled in his face, which was as red as a boiled crawfish, his blue eyes protruding past his wide-open lids. He tried to speak, but I had too much pressure on his throat. I shoved a little harder, then I let go.

His hand flew up to his neck, he coughed, he breathed.

I was back in his face. "Did you tell Solarno that Callahan killed Myra?" He nodded, massaging his throat. "You stupid coward! You told him, but you didn't tell me." I moved to get away from him. "What did you think, that it didn't matter if I died, just another piece of scum, like Solarno, like Myra?" My right hand was balled into a fist. I grabbed it with my left to keep from hitting him.

He spoke with some difficulty. "I thought telling Solarno was what got him killed." He tried to muffle a cough. "I didn't know he had any evidence."

"He had it all along." I sneered at him. "But he wasn't going to give it to you until it failed to get him back in with Callahan. And what would *you* have done with it? With all you've known all these years, you *still* wouldn't tackle Callahan—what?—because of some tapes he has that might ruin your precious standing in the community?"

I stopped to get myself under control. "Did Callahan do it himself?" I asked. He wouldn't look at me, but he nodded once. "What did he think, that Angelesi told Myra about him—that he was in on the take, too? I would have thought he was smart enough to realize that Angelesi would only have bragged about himself, especially while he was in bed with someone he'd paid for."

I knew Myra would have told me if Angelesi had ever mentioned Callahan. The silver seal had miscalculated that one; he had committed a murder for no reason. No wonder he'd been so smug with me—if I hadn't come along, he might have had to invent me.

I said to Richard, "You don't have a choice anymore. You're going to help me go after him."

He put his head in his hands. "I can't." He sounded close to tears. "It will break me. I can't do it."

I was about to start yelling again, but there was a movement off to the side. I whipped around.

I didn't even know she was in the house, but Paula Cotton came into the room, her skin a whiter shade of its usual pale, her blonde hair tossed as if she'd been in bed.

Her voice was unemotional, her words final as death. "Yes you can, Richard. And you will."

32
Epilogue

Chance Callahan found Leonard Yastovich's body in the trunk of his car, which is where Quiro had put it. Quiro hadn't been out to get Yastovich; he had followed me from the Decatur Street motel where he'd been waiting to get Mr. D., and he'd killed Yastovich to save me, because I was such a Good Samaritan (fixing broken windows at the Cotton house, and, generally, looking out for Richard Cotton). But when he did that, it became the first part of his plan to terrorize Callahan, maybe even to murder him, and it had spooked the silver seal badly. It hadn't been necessary for Quiro to know why Richard Cotton was scared of Callahan. As a kid, he'd hero-worshiped Cotton; as a man, he loved him, fanatically. Any enemy of Cotton's was his enemy, too.

Quiro, it seemed, was good at saving everyone but himself. He'd gotten a good look at the raspy-voiced psychopath who liked to carve people's faces before he killed them. His name was Thurston, and if Callahan had paid Thurston all the money he'd promised him, he might have gotten away with everything— because the cop who shot the black kid never did crack and neither did Callahan on that subject. Hell, maybe that was another one of those coincidences. Anyway, Thurston stuck around New Orleans for three days trying to see Callahan and get his money. The police picked him up on his way out of town and he spilled his guts. After that, Uncle Roddy took over.

Whenever Uncle Roddy and the old man get together to toss back a few beers now, sooner or later the scene that went down in Callahan's office gets replayed. At this point, the old man knows more about it than Uncle Roddy does. Uncle Roddy plays himself, tough cop armed with the facts and a lot of shrewd bluff, and the old man plays a much too limp-wristed Callahan finally breaking. Whenever I'm invited to one of their beer-drinking sessions, I try to leave before they get started. One thing, though, neither one of them has ever thrown it up to me that I was wrong about Angelesi having Myra killed. Maybe they don't because they know it wouldn't matter anymore.

I'm free from the obsession of Myra's death, and it isn't just because I found out the truth about her murder. I also found out she wasn't the only woman I could love. I still miss her sometimes, but there are no longer any thoughts about the way it could have been, just about the way it was, the good times, along with the reality that Myra lived like she did because she liked living that way—on the edge. I never could have changed her; only growing old would have, if she hadn't self-destructed first.

Even the Euclid isn't so bad these days. The reason I got such fast action when the bathtub upstairs overflowed was because the owners put in a new manager. They're fixing the place up, and now that I'm feeling so settled in, watch it go condo, and I'll have to move, anyway. But I won't go back to the Channel, and, the truth of it is, I would feel as out of place living in the Garden District as Richard Cotton would feel playing pool at Grady's Irish Channel bar.

The Bucktown Tavern is boarded up and in a state of such deterioration that it will probably fall into the lake during the next big blow. The owners were fined a pittance of what they're worth for showing porno flicks, and they did a stretch of time on the narcotics rap. But they're millionaires from a drug scam that disappeared without a trace the night of Callahan's vice raids. Callahan's drug money, though, won't do him any good.

Richard no longer lives in the house in the Garden District. Paula divorced him and lives there alone. Because Richard didn't have to testify against Callahan, and because Paula had no desire for anyone to know she'd married a homosexual, Richard's sexual identity is still his own business. He is, as he has always been, the victim of his own duplicity, giving up his law practice and living like a hermit in Covington. Every once in a while I go over there to make sure he's still with us and drink a glass of port with him.

As for Lee Diamond—that night in front of Richard Cotton's house was the last time I saw her for a long time. We spoke once, and she managed to stay cool and unemotional. I didn't. If you want to get right down to it, that is what we were really arguing about.

When we did finally see each other again, the same spark was there, but the circumstances were different, and—well, let's get into that another time.